THE GROWLER CHRONICLES

BOOK FIVE

PARADISE FALLS

By

J.C. SAMPSON

The Growler Chronicles Books

- Phase One: Run
- Phase Two: Hide
- Phase Three: Fight
- Book Four: The Battle For Paradise
- Book Five: Paradise Falls
- Coming Soon - Book Six : Hellfire

Stand Alone Short Novellas set in the Growler Chronicles' World

- Deacon

Extra Content and News on J.C. Sampson at jcsampson.com

The Growler Chronicles: Book 5

Paradise Falls

By Joseph Sampson

Table of Contents

Prologue

Nothing Beats Being Prepared

Jennifer Polar – Day 3 of the Outbreak,

Cedar Valley, Texas

Jennifer in the Bunker with one of the Billy brothers

Jennifer Polar watched, a mixture of fascination and unease churning in her gut, as her father meticulously counted his patriot buckets of emergency food. *He is in his element*, she thought, *a man whose years of preparation are finally being utilized.* The grim smile that played at the corners of his mouth only served to underscore his hidden glee during the unfolding catastrophe.

Jennifer was conflicted. There was a part of her that secretly wanted to be locked away in a bunker, away from society, away from real life. She could have time for her art, time to read her philosophy books, and time to work on her mental health. That all sounded good, but the problem was that she only had two months' worth of anti-psychotics. She had to lie to the insurance companies, telling them she was going away on vacation; otherwise, she would only have one month's supply of her risperidone.

I'll be okay, she told herself, but she didn't believe it. *If I were okay, I wouldn't still be living at home with Ma and Pa at the age of 27.*

She was a striking woman who looked younger than her age. Her natural beauty was undeniable, with porcelain skin that seemed to glow from within and a complexion that many would envy. She had high cheekbones, a slender nose, and full, pink lips that often curved into a contemplative smile.

She looked at her father. *He is loving it*, she thought, her mind drifting back to the day when her mother had discovered the extent of Pa's prepper spending. The memory of Mama's fury was still fresh, her shrill voice echoing off the walls as she berated him for blowing a staggering $30,000 on a ten-year supply of dried food rations. Pa had been unmoved, his resolve as unshakable as the concrete walls of their bunker. The food, he had argued, was merely the latest addition to his ever-growing stockpile, a complement to the fifty firearms and countless cases of bullets he had amassed over the years.

Pa, she thought with a pang, *he is a good man, but he has his foibles.* She thought back to the times Pa had come and rescued her when her mind had gotten away from her. Every time she had lapsed into psychosis, he had been there to rescue her, no matter how far he had to travel or at what ungodly time of day the cops had called.

When she first heard news of the outbreak, she had turned to Pa to ask if it was real, or if she was having a delusion. Pa had nodded grimly. “It’s real alright my princess.” But life did not seem to change much for the first two days. It was all some crazy California issue. Then it had been an issue for Arizona and Oregon and Nevada.

Yesterday had been the first time Jennifer had seen the local community begin to panic at the spread of the outbreak.

She and Pa had driven the winding road from their isolated home, Pa's truck kicking up dust as they descended into Cedar Valley. Pa didn't really need anything from town, but he thought it would be good to have extra supplies, if there were any to be had.

Even from a distance, they could tell something was off with the town. The usual sleepy calm of their small town had been replaced by a frenetic energy that set Jennifer's nerves on edge.

That had been the moment that she had realized the outbreak was real…really real…not like all the fantasies Pa had had in the past. Pa had been convinced that Covid was a communist plot to kill all Americans. He had also been convinced that 5G towers were Chinese listening posts. "They're going to invade!" Pa had assured the family as he bought more boxes of ammo. "They're gonna' find a gun behind every blade of grass."

Jennifer had often worried that her father might suffer from the same delusions that she suffered from during her episodes.

This time, his paranoid delusions were being televised 24 hours a day on the news in ultra-high definition. The dead sprinted down the streets of Oakland, California, tearing the living apart.

She had not felt any fear those first two days.

Now, chaos was coming to Texas. Cedar Valley Main Street was a scene of barely controlled panic. The local Walmart's parking lot overflowed, cars haphazardly parked on curbs and grass. People streamed in and out, arms laden with supplies. Jennifer glimpsed shelves being stripped bare. A woman clutched a case of water to her chest like a shield while two men grappled over canned goods.

Jennifer had subconsciously rested her hand on Pa's arm as he drove. She wanted the contact for comfort. Pa was strong, he would protect her.

"Jesus," Pa muttered, navigating around a fender bender nobody seemed interested in addressing.

At Pete's Gas n' Go, a line of vehicles snaked around the block. As they passed, Jennifer witnessed two men shoving each other by the pumps, their argument escalating rapidly. Nobody intervened; everyone was laser-focused on their own urgent needs.

They pulled into the hardware store's lot. Inside, the usual neighborly atmosphere had evaporated. Mrs. Henderson from church was there, clutching armfuls of batteries and glaring suspiciously at anyone who came too close. Mr. Garcia, who always had a friendly wave, brushed past them without a glance, his cart piled high with tarps and duct tape.

"Ain't got no more water purification tablets," the clerk told Pa apologetically. "No generators neither. Sold the last one an hour ago to Bob Wilson for twice the sticker price. Man was desperate."

Pa chewed his lip pensively. "I guess I got enough. Just was being extra cautious I guess."

As they left empty-handed, Jennifer noticed the Robinson family hurriedly packing their minivan. The parents snapped at each other while their kids watched wide-eyed from the backseat.

"Where you folks headin'?" Pa called out, but Mr. Robinson just shook his head, avoiding eye contact as they sped away.

"Alright," said Pa and looked at Jennifer. "Now we'll go to the Billy Brothers' and see if they have any more patriot supplies. Then it's home."

That had been just yesterday, and now Jennifer realized that she might never go to town again. *How long will we be in the bunker?* She shivered at the thought that the bunker was going to be her new home. *It may as well be a prison.*

She looked around the bunker, clenching and unclenching her fists. Her breaths started to become slightly more shallow and more rapid. Again she tried to think of the bunker as a good thing. *We'll be safe. I can read. We'll be safe.*

The outside world will be gone, she thought. *All I have is Ma, Pa, and Junior.*

Her hand stroked the walls. She had watched the workmen build it and knew the walls were thick, reinforced concrete, cold to the touch, and painted a dull, industrial gray. Shelves lined the perimeter, stocked with the patriot buckets of emergency food her father had so meticulously collected over the years. The sight of them now brought her no comfort because they represented just how long they could be locked away from the world.

I could be imprisoned here all my life, but then what is so good about the outside world anyway. She had wanted a husband, a family, but who in her right mind would have her, knowing the episodes she was prone to. "Never stick your dick in crazy," one boy had sneered at her.

How could she argue with that. *I'm okay of I take my meds… well usually anyway.*

In one corner, she noticed a small table cluttered with scattered papers, a few half-empty bottles of water, and a radio.

Despite the bunker door being wide open, the air was stale, filled with the faint, lingering scent of dried food and disinfectant. It was musty. *I bet there's mold,* she thought. The fluorescent lights above cast a harsh, unwelcoming glow, amplifying every shadow and making the bunker feel even more claustrophobic.

Her gaze drifted to the bunker door, a massive steel barrier that would separate her from the world outside. *That cost a fortune. Pa's prepper obsession was an expensive hobby.*

Now, as the bunker TV droned on in the background, painting a grim picture of the chaos and destruction wrought by the outbreak in California, she was suddenly brought out of her dreamlike state by a new report. "A state of Emergency has been declared across the whole state of Texas. The National Guard has been deployed..." The picture faded out to static for a few seconds, then returned. "…a mandatory curfew..." The picture turned to static for a few more seconds and returned once more. "…and the governor assures all citizens that the rolling blackouts currently sweeping throughout the state will be rapidly remediated and there is no need for panic, absolutely zero need for …" The screen went blank.

The realization hit Jennifer that society was ending. That all the safety, all the joys and pleasures of modern civilization had just ended. She felt tears welling up. Earlier, she had thought of the bunker as a refuge, but now it suddenly felt like a hospice. *I am too young. I haven't lived. I don't have the mental health needed to be locked up with my family for years. I'd rather die.*

She pouted, on the verge of crying, but then she stifled the building sob. *I'm not a kid. I don't want to be a burden to Pa and Ma.*

Junior nonchalantly changed the channel. The next channel was still active. A shaky cell phone video filled the screen, showing growling, shambling creatures roaming the streets of a city. The footage cut to a frantic reporter outside a makeshift government command center. "The situation is deteriorating rapidly," she shouted over the sound of distant screams and sirens. "Despite the governor's assurances just hours ago, the containment measures have failed. The infected are overrunning the quarantine zones."

Jennifer's phone buzzed with social media notifications. A friend in San Diego posted, "OMG, they're breaking through the barricades! Military's pulling out. We're on our own now. #Apocalypse #PrayForUs." Another update from a cousin in Fresno read, "Evacuation gridlock. People abandoning cars. Infected everywhere. This can't be real."

The news anchor's voice trembled as they reported on the federal government's response. "The President has authorized the use of military force to establish safe zones, but reports from the ground suggest it may be too little, too late. Professor Preston of the CDC admits they're overwhelmed, with no clear understanding of how the infection spreads or how to stop it."

These nightmarish scenes of death and destruction were being played out mostly on the West Coast, but they were spreading, and now even mighty Texas was being hit. Yet here, Pa seemed more alive than ever, his eyes glinting with a strange mix of excitement and satisfaction. As the nation descended into chaos, he stood, a grim smile playing at the corners of his mouth, as if to say, "I told you so."

They watched the news presenter struggle to maintain her composure. Pa's enjoyment was growing. Oh, he tried to hide it, to maintain a veneer of solemnity, but Jennifer could see right through the façade. This was what he had been waiting for, the moment when all his years of preparation would finally pay off. Ma was strangely quiet. *She must be frightened,* Jennifer realized. *She is hoping against hope that Pa knows what to do. She just wants her children to be safe.*

"It's a terrible thing," Pa said, shaking his head with a smile. "But some of us saw it coming. Well, maybe not *this* exactly, but we knew something was coming. And we, the prepared, are going to be in damn good shape now that the shit has—pardon my French—hit the mother fucking fan."

Her mind drifted again to the previous day's visit to the Billy brothers' Patriot Supply store. She had accompanied her father, more out of boredom than interest, but now those memories took on a sinister new light.

The store had been busier than she'd ever seen it, packed with panicked customers frantically grabbing supplies off the shelves. Jennifer had noticed Joe Billy at the counter, his usual jovial demeanor replaced by a calculating gleam in his eyes as he tallied up exorbitant totals for desperate shoppers.

"Supply and demand, folks," he'd said with a shrug when one customer complained about the prices. "Ain't our fault you waited till the last minute to prep."

As her father loaded up their cart, Jennifer wandered toward the back of the store. Behind a partially open office door, she overheard two of the younger Billy brothers in hushed conversation, but she only caught pieces of what was said.

"Just doing the math, the Polar family are the ones…."

"…he's here again today…"

"…their bunker is the biggest…"

"…wouldn't take much…"

They had chuckled darkly.

She remembered, too, the way Joe's eyes had lingered on their fully stocked cart as they checked out, the way his smile hadn't quite reached his eyes when he'd clapped her father on the back and said, "You're all set now, old friend. Nothin' to worry about."

Jennifer shivered. She told herself she was reading too much into things, letting the stress of the situation get to her. The Billy brothers were friends, allies in this crazy new world. They'd never do anything to hurt her family.

She had considered telling her Pa, but she wasn't sure what she had really heard, and she had a history of being prone to paranoid delusions. It had started in high school. It had started small. She always thought people were plotting against her. She thought the police were following her. Two years ago, she had become convinced that a man was stalking her, and somehow, she just knew he would kidnap her, that she would be put in the crazy man's cellar and tortured for the rest of her life. The fear had built up inside her to the point she wanted to die. She had no idea where these intrusive thoughts had come from, but they were incessant and had led her to attempt suicide.

No, I will not let intrusive thoughts in, she thought, trying to stop thinking about the Billy Brothers.

The drive home had been tense and quiet. Jennifer stared out the window at the familiar landscape, the dense trees and scattered farmhouses that separated them from town. She'd always loved their secluded home, but now that isolation took on a new, almost ominous meaning.

"Pa," she finally broke the silence, "what's going to happen to everyone?"

Her father's grip tightened on the steering wheel. "Not our concern, Jen. We prepared. We're ready. That's all that matters now."

As their house came into view, Jennifer couldn't shake the unease that had settled in her stomach. The world she knew was unraveling at an alarming speed, and she wondered how much worse it could get, even here in their rural sanctuary.

She dreaded thinking about what the town looked like now. Yesterday, there had still been some semblance of order, but now, as she stood in the bunker, she realized civilization itself was dying.

"They're calling them growlers," Junior chimed in, his eyes wide with a mix of fear and fascination. Jennifer's younger brother had always been more receptive to Pa's prepper mindset, eagerly soaking up every lesson and piece of advice their father had to offer.

It didn't seem real to Jennifer as she watched her father and brother bond over the unfolding apocalypse. The world outside their bunker was changing in ways she had never imagined, and even with all of Pa's preparation, she couldn't help but wonder if they were truly ready for what lay ahead.

And what of everyone else? Dennis, the boy in the supermarket who smiled so nicely at her.

Pa made a mark in his notebook. "That's because the mainstream media don't want to call them zombies, which is, let's face it, what they are… but zombies doesn't sound credible now does it?"

"How long before the growlers get here, Pa?" asked Junior with a hint of excitement.

"Don't know," said Pa. "But we'll be safe and sound in our bunker, and let me tell you, nothing is getting in there. Now, you two kids, finish taking the food down, and I'll lock up. You say goodbye to the world now."

"What about my birthday?" asked Jennifer. "I guess I don't get a party, but can we at least go to…"

"We're not going anywhere," said Pa. "Ma has baked a cake; we'll have it in the bunker."

"But there ain't no growlers around here in Texas," said Jennifer.

Pa seemed to think for a moment. "No, we are going into lockdown now, before it's too late. There are growlers in Arizona. It may only be another day or two before they arrive here in Cedar Valley. When you see them running down our Valley Vista Rd, then it's already too late."

"Do what your Pa says," said Ma. "Take the food down."

Pa nodded. "I think I have a box of shells in the shed; I'm going to grab them, and then I'll join you and lock the bunker door."

It took five minutes to take the last of the food down. Junior added his secret stash of candies, which he had in his closet. When everything was in the bunker, Jennifer prepared herself mentally for the door to be closed. *Is there anything else I should grab before they close the door?* She fiddled nervously with her hair, rolling it between her fingers.

The bunker was in their storm cellar. Pa had built it, with the help of the Billy brothers, when Obama was elected, which Pa said was the beginning of the end of the world. The Billy brothers belonged to the Patriot's militia, and they were adamant that everyone who called themselves a patriot be prepared for Armageddon. They had a supply store that specialized in bunker preparation materials. The sign above it said "Patriot Supplies". They sold buckets of emergency food, bunker plans, guns, ammunition, and everything you could want for your patriot bunker.

Once a month, the militia would meet to discuss survival tactics. "Nothing beats being prepared" was their motto.

I guess they were right, thought Jennifer as she stared at the open bunker door.

"You father is taking a long time to get those shells," said Ma. "Can you ask him if he needs some help?"

"Yes, Ma," Jennifer agreed. She was happy to have an excuse to go out and say a last goodbye to the outside world. She ran out of the bunker, up the cellar stairs, and out into the garden. She immediately saw her Pa lying flat on the ground next to the shed.

"What are you doing, Pa?" she asked, running up to him.

There was a pool of blood under his head.

A surge of fear pulsed through her. "Pa!" she shouted and knelt next to him, putting her hand on his back. "Pa!" *Oh my God! Oh my God! Oh my God!*

There was a tiny hole in his head at his left temple. She grabbed his head and lifted it but immediately dropped it again when she saw a much larger hole in his right temple. She spotted a strange grey chunk of matter on the ground. Her heart seemed to freeze. *That's brain.*

"Hey Jennifer," said a voice behind her. She whirled around, standing up in the process. It was Joe Billy, one of the Billy brothers.

"Somethings happened to Pa, you gotta help!" she pleaded, her voice shaking so badly she could barely make the words comprehensible. She noticed three other Billy brothers entering her home. He brow furrowed. "What's going on?" she asked in a voice made hoarse by fear and grief.

"You better come with me," Joe said, gesturing for her to approach.

His voice was to calm and had an edge to it that seemed almost malign. She did not want to leave Pa. Her heart felt like, somehow, Pa needed her, but she saw the gun in Joe's hand. Her already racing heart picked up its pace and thumped so hard against her chest she could actually hear it. She looked at Pa, or what had once been he Pa. *He's gone.*

He looked at Joe's pocked face. Where was his concern? Why did he have the edges of a grin. Her gaze crept down and finally locked onto the muzzle of his gun. Was it smoking? His eyes moved from her to Pa and then back to her. Then his eyes did that thing that boys do, they travelled down her body, appraising and lingering.

Now? She shook her head. *Now?*

"I said you better come with me," he repeated and raised his gun.

Only then, in that moment, understanding came to her. He had done this to Pa. He was a monster. He had done this to Pa and then he had stood there and undressed her with his eyes. Her fists clenched. All semblance of logic fled her mind. She screamed and ran at him intent on clawing out his eyes and scratching and biting him until he begged for mercy and she wouldn't stop until he too lay in a pool of blood.

Joe chuckled, and dodged. Her charged missed and he managed to swat her backside with his right hand as she passed him. She fell to the floor and immediately rose to charge again but he pushed her back down. She snarled at him but slowly she understood that she was physically no match for him.

She stared into his eyes with all the venom in her dark heart.

"I will not ask you again," he said and pushed the barrel of his gun into her forehead.

She took a deep shuddering breath, swallowed and slowly with gritted teeth stood ready to obey him.

The sound of gunfire came from inside her home.

"What's happening!" she shouted and started to run forward. Joe Billy pointed a gun at her and tried to grab her shirt, but she pulled clear, desperate to join Ma and Junior.

"Stop!" shouted Joe.

She didn't care about his stupid gun; she sprinted to the house, pushed the door open, and ran inside and down to the bunker. Ma was lying face up, a hole in her chest. *She's dead!* Junior was just behind her with half his head missing.

This can't be real. This can't be real. That's it! It's one of my delusions. Nothing is real. Nothing is real.

The Billy brothers hoisted the bodies onto their shoulders and took them outside.

Joe pushed Jennifer inside the bunker.

Don't let this be real. God, let this be a delusion. Please, please, please, please, please, please. Oh God, please.

"What is going on?" she screamed. She could not understand what had happened. The Billy brothers were good ole boys. Everyone liked them. They were always the life of the party. *They could not have done this. Why have they done this? They could not have done this. Why!*

The bunker TV was broadcasting local news. "We have reports coming in that a riot has broken out in Austin and has already spread to the western suburbs…."

"That is what's happening," said Joe. "That California shit has come to Texas."

Jennifer stared at him with wild eyes. "But why do this to a fellow patriot?" her voice was barely above a whisper.

The rest of the Billy brothers returned, along with their other kin folk, their mother, father, sister, and a couple of cousins.

"I am sorry, Jennifer, baby doll, your Pa was really well prepared. He paid us to help him build the biggest bunker in town. Then he bought more patriot buckets than anyone else in town. Then, he bought more ammo than anyone else in town. In short, he was the most prepared. We took his money, but we also took notes. If the shit goes down, and you ain't prepared, then you better find someone who *is* prepared and take all their shit. That's what we're doing, baby doll."

She beat her fists on his chest, but he almost did not notice. "But you guys should be prepared. You were preaching about it for years."

"Well, honey," said Joe, stroking a wisp of hair out of her eyes. "We were making a quick buck. We never thought anything like this was actually going to happen. The last few days, we plum-sold our entire repository. Then we realized we might actually need a well-supplied bunker, so…here we are."

"But you killed my whole family?" she screamed.

"Well, honey child, what use would they be to us?" he said with a malign grin. "Just mouths to feed."

The news report showed growlers running down streets until they knocked over the camera, and then the view was just of blue sky.

She looked behind Joe as the older Billy brothers were closing the thick bunker door. The whole Billy family was settling in. Her heart ached at the sudden loss of everyone she loved. She realized she'd rather die with them than live on without them. She wanted them to put a bullet in her brain.

"Well, If Ma, Pa, and Junior were of no use, then I am of no use either," she said. "You'd best be putting a bullet in my head."

Joe stroked her hair. "Oh, honey child, we'll find a use for you."

Day 130, Cedar Valley, Texas

Months later, Jennifer was lying on her small cot, the one that had been meant for Junior; she was staring mindlessly at the bunker ceiling. Her thoughts had become increasingly numb since her world had ended, and this new nightmare existence had begun.

She had neglected to take her anti-psychotics, after all, what was the point. Madness might be preferable to sanity. Any delusion would be better than reality.

The early days had been a blur of grief and fear. She'd barely eaten, barely slept. Every time she closed her eyes, she saw Pa's body, saw the light leave Junior's eyes. The Billy family had tried to act like regular people, as if they were all one big happy family now. They'd invite her to meals, to game nights. She'd refused at first, but hunger and loneliness eventually wore her down.

The Billy brothers, Joe, Jesse, and Ray, and their sixteen-year-old cousin, Dale Billy, showed no remorse for their actions.

She remembered the first time Joe Billy had looked at her with that predatory gleam in his eye. "Time to earn your keep, baby doll," he'd drawled, reaching for her. She'd recoiled, pressing herself against the wall, heart pounding.

No! Don't think of bad things. Think of times at Aunt Cassie's farm, riding horses, petting goats.

All the brothers, even Dale, had taken their turns with her. She had looked at Ma Billy for help, but she had just smiled and shook her head as if to say, "Boys will be boys." Their Memaw had the grace to look uncomfortable and turn away, but that was it.

No! Don't think of bad things.

One memory stood out starkly. About a week after the takeover, she'd been sitting at the table, listlessly pushing food around her plate. Memaw Billy had reached out, patting her hand. "There, there, dear. You'll see. This is all for the best. We're safer together." Jennifer had looked up, meeting the old woman's eyes, and for a moment, she'd seen genuine kindness there. It had broken something in her. She'd fled the table, retching in the bathroom, horrified that for just a second, she'd felt grateful to one of her family's killers.

Jennifer's nails scraped against the bunker wall, leaving faint red streaks where her skin broke. The pain barely registered. Her eyes reflected in the bathroom mirror were sunken and haunted, darting between the shadows cast by the harsh fluorescent lights. Every flicker made her flinch, phantom gunshots echoing in her mind.

Nights brought no respite. She'd wake, drenched in sweat, sheets tangled around her legs like grasping hands. The metallic taste of blood filled her mouth where she'd bitten her tongue to keep from screaming. In those moments between sleep and waking, she'd reach out, expecting to feel Junior's warm presence beside her. The emptiness that greeted her fingers was a void that threatened to swallow her whole.

During the day, she would catch glimpses of herself in reflective surfaces. A stranger stared back, all jutting bones and matted hair.

Sometimes, she'd lock eyes with this gaunt specter and feel a surge of something primal. Her fists would clench, nails biting into her palms until tiny crescents of blood welled up. The pain was an anchor, a reminder that she was still here, still fighting, even if only against herself.

At mealtimes, the scent of food turned her stomach. She'd force down tasteless mouthfuls, imagining each bite was poison. Across the table, Joe Billy's laughter boomed. Jennifer's hand tightened around her fork, knuckles white. For a moment, she saw herself leaping across the table, driving the utensil deep into his throat. The fantasy was so vivid she could almost feel the warm spurt of blood on her face. Then reality reasserted itself, leaving her trembling and nauseous.

In rare moments of solitude, she would press her forehead against the cool metal of the bunker door. She'd run her fingers along the seams, searching for weaknesses that didn't exist. There was a key needed to unlock the door, and Joe kept it on his belt. Sometimes, she'd whisper to the unyielding walls, a litany of promises and pleas. "I'll kill them all, Pa. I swear it. Just give me strength. Please, God, give me strength."

As weeks bled into months, her hatred became a living thing, coiling in her gut like a venomous snake. She'd lie awake, staring at the ceiling, imagining elaborate scenarios of revenge. In her mind's eye, she saw the Billy family writhing in agony, begging for mercy she'd never grant. These violent fantasies were both balm and torment, offering a twisted comfort even as they reminded her of her utter powerlessness.

One day, while helping prepare dinner, Jennifer found herself alone in the kitchen. Her gaze fell on the knife block. Without conscious thought, her hand reached out, fingers closing around the handle of the largest blade. The weight of it felt right, promising. For a heartbeat, she savored the possibility. Then footsteps approached, and the moment shattered. She returned the knife, hands shaking, knowing that her chance would come. It had to. The alternative was unthinkable.

She had learned to survive. She'd built walls around her heart and learned to smile and nod at the right times, all while nurturing the ember of revenge that burned deep within her. She became a ghost in the bunker, trying to avoid being seen. Never brushing her hair, never applying deodorant, refusing to wash, wearing clothes that hid her curves and chest, she bided her time and waited for a chance—any chance—to make the Billy family pay for what they'd done.

She imagined various scenarios where she could exact her revenge on the Billy family. In her fantasies, she saw herself using her father's hunting knife, hidden beneath her mattress, to silently dispatch them one by one. The thought brought a grim satisfaction, but she knew it was just that – a thought, a fantasy. Could she ever find the courage to act upon it? *Even if I did kill them, then what? I just stay in this bunker with their corpses, hiding from the dead outside.*

This is not the first time I have suffered. I will survive this.

She had suffered in the past, a time in her life her family never spoke of. The memories had become foggy over time. She remembered waking up in the sterile hospital room, her wrists bandaged, the beep of monitors mocking her failed attempt. Then came the institution—stark white walls, group therapy sessions, and the constant scrutiny of well-meaning but detached professionals. Most of the time, she had walked the grounds, her wrists itching and tears streaming down her cheeks.

The other patients, with their vacant stares and trembling hands, had terrified her. She'd felt so out of place, so misunderstood. Aunt Cassie had visited her most often, bringing books and whispering strange, comforting stories about secret underground worlds where pain couldn't reach. That had been the time she learned that Aunt Cassie was really her half-sister, that her mother had had other men in her life other than Jennifer's father. Even after learning Cassie was her sister, she still called her Aunt Cassie.

Cassie had done something to her in the facility, something Jennifer could not quite remember, something that did not make sense at the time… something that helped. Jennifer had clung to those visits, to Cassie's unwavering presence, like a lifeline. She still longed for the comfort of Cassie's scent. Cassie wore a very distinctive perfume.

When Jeniffer was finally released, she'd promised her family, and more importantly, herself, that she'd never be that weak again. Now, trapped in this bunker hell, that promise was tested daily.

It was all so meaningless, she thought remembering her past episodes of depression. *I had no reason to be sad. My mind rebelled against itself. But it was for the best, for I learned to be strong.*

She focused her mind on happier times, memories that now felt like they belonged to someone else's life. She remembered her twenty-seventh birthday, just weeks before the outbreak. Pa had surprised her with a used pickup truck, its faded red paint gleaming in the Texas sun. "Every ranch girl needs her own wheels," he'd said, tossing her the keys with a proud grin. She'd spent that afternoon driving down dusty back roads with Junior, windows down, country music blaring, feeling invincible.

There were times when Aunt Cassie showed her how to get boys. Boys that Jennifer could never keep for long, but who needs a boy for long?

Then there was the county fair last summer. The scent of funnel cakes and the distant squeal of rides mingled with the earthy smell of livestock. She'd won a blue ribbon for her apple pie, Ma beaming beside her as the judge pinned it on. *Can you believe it… me baking pies.* She had ridden the Ferris wheel, and later, she'd ridden Tommy Baker, her heart racing faster than any carnival ride could make it.

These golden memories stood like a seawall against the nightmare that followed the Billy family's betrayal.

A deep, guttural cough echoed through the bunker, snapping Jennifer out of her dark reverie. She sat up, curiosity piqued despite herself. The cough came again, followed by concerned murmurs from the Billy family.

"Memaw? You alright?" one of the brothers called out.

Jennifer crept to the edge of her secluded corner, peering around to see the Billy clan gathered around their elderly matriarch.

Memaw Billy looked pale, her breathing labored as she waved off her family's concerns.

"Just a tickle," Memaw wheezed. "Nothing to fuss about."

Jennifer could see the worry etched on the faces of the Billy family. Memaw was old, and in this new world, any illness could be a death sentence. As she watched the family's anxious hovering, a small, dark part of Jennifer hoped that this might be the end for the old woman. It wasn't much, but it would be something—a crack in the Billy family's armor, a small taste of the loss they had inflicted on her.

The day dragged on, tension building in the confined space of the bunker. Jennifer retreated to her cot, pretending to sleep while keeping one ear tuned to the whispered conversations and Memaw's increasingly labored breathing.

As night fell—or what passed for night in the timeless confines of the bunker—Jennifer was jolted awake by a sudden commotion. Cries of alarm and the sound of hurried footsteps filled the air as the Billy family rushed to Memaw's side.

"She can't breathe!" someone shouted. "Do something!"

Jennifer sat up, her heart racing as she watched the scene unfold. Memaw Billy was thrashing on her bed, gasping for air, her face turning an alarming shade of blue. The family's attempts to help seemed futile, their panic palpable in the enclosed space, and then, as suddenly as it had begun, it was over. Memaw Billy gave one final, rattling breath and went still.

For a long moment, no one moved. Then, slowly, the reality seemed to set in. The mother began to sob quietly while the brothers stood in stunned silence. Jennifer watched as the initial shock gave way to grim practicality.

"We can't keep her here," one of the brothers said, his voice hoarse. "In this heat...it won't be long before..."

The implication hung in the air. A decaying body in their enclosed space would quickly become a health hazard. Jennifer listened as they debated what to do, a part of her marveling at the surreal nature of the situation. Here she was, eavesdropping on her family's murderers as they planned a makeshift funeral.

As the discussion continued, something caught Jennifer's eye. A twitch. Small, almost imperceptible, but definitely there. Memaw's head had moved.

Jennifer's breath caught in her throat. She remembered the information from the President's website, the warnings about the Black and its effects. Those who died from it didn't stay dead. They came back as growlers.

For a moment, Jennifer considered speaking up, warning the Billy family, but the memory of her own family's brutal murder stilled her tongue. *Let them face the consequences of their actions*, she thought bitterly. *Maybe Memaw would take one of them down with her.*

The twitching increased. Jennifer watched, heart pounding, as Memaw's body began to convulse. The Billy family, caught up in their planning, didn't notice at first. It wasn't until Memaw suddenly sat bolt upright that chaos erupted.

Screams filled the bunker as the reanimated Memaw launched herself at the nearest person—her young nephew. Jennifer's eyes widened in shock as the boy went down, Memaw's teeth sinking into his back. Jennifer hadn't meant for a child to be hurt—her anger was directed at the adults, not an innocent kid.

The Billy brothers sprang into action, trying to pull their transformed grandmother off the screaming boy. In the struggle, Jennifer saw each of them receive bites and scratches from the frenzied Memaw.

Finally, with a cry of anguish, the mother raised a gun and fired. Memaw Billy collapsed, truly dead this time.

The bunker was a cacophony of panic and pain as the Billy brothers staggered, clutching their wounds. Memaw's body lay crumpled on the floor, her lifeless form a grotesque pile of shattered flesh.

Joe Billy was the first to collapse into a chair; his hand pressed against a deep bite wound on his forearm. Jesse, Ray, and Dale followed suit, each nursing their own injuries with pained grimaces.

"Ma!" Joe called out, his voice strained with both pain and fear. "Get the first aid kit! We need help!"

Ma, a woman who had seen her fair share of hardship, rushed into the back room. She returned and paused.

"Oh my God." She gasped, dropping to her knees beside Joe. Her hands shook as she reached for a white bandage, trying to staunch the blood flowing from his wound.

"Memaw," Joe growled through clenched teeth. "I can't believe how she came at us like a damn wild animal. She always loved and looked after us, and now… she bit all of us."

Jesse, who had a nasty bite on his shoulder, winced as he tried to adjust his position. "It happened so fast... We didn't see it coming."

Ray was uncharacteristically silent, his face pale as he stared at the bite on his thigh. Dale, sitting next to him, looked down at the gouge on his hand, his usually calm demeanor replaced with a trembling fear.

Jennifer looked at Dale's wound. *I could suggest they amputate. He might survive. He is just a kid, after all… but he was old enough to rape me… let him die.*

Ma worked frantically, applying bright white bandages to bind the wounds. Her breath came in short, sharp bursts. "It's okay, boys. We'll clean these up, and you'll be fine. Just...just like any other injury. Right? You're strong. You'll pull through."

She doesn't believe that. She knows what comes next. She's seen enough on the emergency broadcasts.

After a few minutes, Jennifer noticed the boys were already showing telltale signs: the unnatural pallor of their skin, the feverish sweat already beading on their foreheads, and the dull glaze settling over their eyes.

"Ma," Jesse whispered, his voice barely above a croak. "We're not gonna make it, are we?"

Ma froze, her hands hovering above his wound; the truth of his words must have set in like a stone in her chest. Tears welled up in her eyes as she looked at the boy who had had so much potential, so much unlived life.

Her eyes shifted from his wound to the floor. "No," she whispered, her voice trembling. "No, I won't let it happen. You'll fight it. You have to. You're my boys..."

Joe reached out, his hand finding hers, his grip weak but determined. "Ma...it's over. We know it. You know it. Just...just stay with us, alright? Don't leave us alone."

Why is he asking her to do that? He knows they'll become growlers and attack. Why would he want that?

A look of understanding passed between Joe and his Ma.

What kind of life would she have stuck in a bunker with only her dead sons and mother? She is ready to die with them.

Ma nodded, choking back a sob as she knelt between them, clutching Joe's hand in one of hers and reaching out to touch Jesse's shoulder with the other.

For a long, agonizing moment, the bunker was silent except for the ragged breaths of the boys.

One by one, the boys began to slip away. Their breathing grew shallow, their bodies slackened, and the light faded from their eyes.

In the eerie quiet that followed the last boy's death, Ma Billy turned to Jennifer, her eyes wild with a mixture of grief and fury. She raised the gun, pointing it directly at Jennifer's head.

"You," she snarled. "You knew, didn't you? I saw you looking at Memaw's body. You could have warned us!"

Jennifer backed away, her hands raised. "I...I didn't know for sure."

Ma prodded the gun toward her head. "The boys will come back as those beast things, and when they do, you'll be their first meal."

Jennifer was forced back to her cot at gunpoint, her mind racing. This wasn't how she had imagined her revenge. With a final prod from the gun, she sat on her cot and waited. They both knew it would not be long before the boys would come for them. They could not see the bodies from the bedroom.

It was so … satisfying watching them die. Who would have known that witnessing death could be so … enjoyable?

Later, there was a shuffling sound from the main room where the boys' bodies lay.

"Stand up," the mother commanded Jennifer. "It's time. Stand by the entrance. I will have the satisfaction of seeing you be their first meal.

Jennifer rose on shaky legs, her eyes darting between the doorway into the main room and the gun aimed at her head. *This is it*, she thought. *This is how I die.* A thought occurred that the gun might be an easier death than being torn apart by the boys' teeth, but she dismissed the thought.

A horrific, tortuous death is what I deserve. I am a terrible person.

"Come on, boys," shouted Ma. "Dinner time."

A series of sinister howls filled Jennifer's ears. Then came the growls. They sounded like they came from primordial beasts. *Why do they growl like that.* A memory began to surface. She had heard that growl before somewhere. Somewhere dark. Somewhere secret. She could not fully surface the memory. It clung to the edges of her mind, and like a dream, the more she tried to remember it, the more it faded.

Joe Billy appeared in the doorway. His eyes were milky white, and black goop seeped from his mouth. His black teeth were barred in a silent snarl. For a moment, his eyes focused on Jennifer, but then they looked past her, as if she were not even there.

The other boys appeared behind Joe. They had all turned into beasts.

Joe's milky eyes fixed on Ma, a guttural growl rumbling from deep in his chest. Without warning, he lunged forward, brushing past Jennifer as if she were nothing more than a ghost. His teeth, still human but driven by inhuman hunger, sank into Ma's throat. Her scream pierced the air, high and shrill, before dissolving into a wet, gurgling sound.

Jennifer's breath started coming in short, sharp gasps. She pressed herself against the wall, eyes wide and unblinking, unable to look away from the horror unfolding before her.

Jesse and Ray converged on Ma's thrashing body, their once-familiar faces twisted into snarls of pure animal rage. Jesse latched onto her arm, teeth tearing through flesh. The crack of bone echoed in the bunker, and Jennifer flinched, her nails digging into her palms hard enough to draw blood.

Ma's eyes locked onto Jennifer's for a moment. There was a momentary expression of incomprehension in her terrified glare before the pain and horror overtook her.

Ray buried his face in Ma's abdomen, ripping through cloth and skin. The wet sound of entrails being torn free filled the air, and Jennifer's stomach lurched. The acrid taste of bile rose in her throat, but she swallowed it back, her eyes never leaving the gruesome scene.

As Dale, the youngest, clamped his jaws around Ma's leg, a strange sensation rippled through Jennifer. The growls, the snarls, the tearing of flesh - it all seemed eerily familiar. *That memory again.* It tickled the edges of her mind, dark and elusive. *I was underground somewhere with these … growling creatures. I remember fear.* But as she grasped for the memory, it slipped away again, leaving her with nothing but a vague sense of déjà vu and a cold sweat on her brow.

Ma's eyes darted between her sons' faces, until again, her gaze locked with Jennifer's for a moment, silently pleading for help. Jennifer stared back, her breath catching in her throat. A small, dark part of her whispered, "Good. Let her suffer."

Then she screamed. "Suffer! Suffer! You are all demons. Hell has come and you are demons."

The metallic scent of blood filled the air, mixing with the stench of voided bowels. Jennifer's nostrils flared, drinking in the scent. Her lips twitched, fighting against the inappropriate urge to smile.

Ma screamed.

"Yes!" shouted Jennifer. "Scream! Scream until your lungs burst." She spat the words. She felt froth in her own mouth.

Ma's screams devolved into agonized whimpers, punctuated by the wet sounds of tearing flesh. Her body twitched and spasmed as the monsters that were once her sons continued their relentless assault. Blood pooled on the floor, spreading outward in a dark, viscous puddle that lapped at Jennifer's feet.

Jennifer watched, transfixed, as the light slowly faded from Ma's eyes. Even after Ma had long since stopped moving, the growlers continued to feed. The sound of their feasting - the ripping, the chewing, the wet smacking of lips - filled Jennifer's ears.

A laugh bubbled up from deep within her chest, starting as a small giggle and growing into a hysterical cackle. She laughed until tears streamed down her face, her body shaking uncontrollably. The laughter echoed off the bunker walls, a jarring counterpoint to the growlers' snarls.

As her laughter subsided into hiccuping gasps, Jennifer slid down the wall, her legs no longer able to support her. She sat in stunned silence, watching the creatures that had once been the Billy family shamble aimlessly around the blood-soaked bunker, completely ignoring her presence.

The only sadness in her was because their suffering was over.

"Look at you!" she shouted at them. "That's what you get! Karma's a fucking bitch ain't it."

The growlers moved past her, their milky eyes unseeing, their blackened mouths still dripping with Ma's blood. Jennifer's mind raced, trying to understand why they weren't attacking her. That nagging sense of familiarity tugged at her again - a memory of darkness, of underground spaces, of growlers that didn't see her. But like before, the memory remained frustratingly out of reach, leaving her with more questions than answers.

She laughed again. *I am laughing. I always knew something was wrong with me. I am laughing at this.*

When it was over, the Billy family—her tormentors, her captors—were gone, replaced by mindless growlers that shambled aimlessly around the bunker… ignoring her.

She stood frozen, unable to process what had just happened. *Why are these creatures moving around me as if I am invisible? Never once showing any interest in attacking me.* Slowly, cautiously, she made walked up to Joe and grasped the keys on his belt.

He looked down at her arm, then up to her face. His head tilted and he drew closer until his mouth was an inch from hers. He seemed to be recognizing her. A surge of black liquid spluttered out of his mouth.

She unclipped the keys from the belt and stepped back.

Her hand trembled as she unlocked and turned the heavy wheel of the bunker door. With a hiss of air, it swung open, revealing the familiar confines of her family's basement. Dust motes danced in the dim light filtering through the small, grimy windows.

She paused at the foot of the wooden stairs, her fingers tracing the handrail where Pa's hand had worn a smooth groove over the years. Each step creaked under her weight, a haunting chorus of memories as she ascended.

The basement door opened into the kitchen. Jennifer's breath caught in her throat. Everything was exactly as they'd left it that fateful day.

She moved through the house in a daze, each room a fresh wound. In the living room, where they'd watched movies together, Pa's recliner was still indented with his shape. In her bedroom, posters curled at the edges, and stuffed animals watched with glassy eyes. In Junior's room, model airplanes hang motionless from the ceiling.

Finally, she reached the front door. She placed her hand on the knob, took a deep breath, and stepped out into the blinding Texas sunlight. The porch boards creaked beneath her feet as her eyes adjusted to the glare.

And there they were, dozens of growlers shambling across the overgrown lawn, weaving between abandoned farm equipment and encroaching wilderness. The familiar landscape of her childhood was now an alien world populated by nightmarish monsters.

As she stood there, frozen between the threshold of her past and this new, terrifying present, Jennifer realized that stepping out of the bunker had been more than just a physical journey. She had crossed an invisible line, leaving behind the last vestiges of her old life and stepping into a world where nothing would ever be the same again.

The long, winding driveway leading to their isolated property was now overgrown, with nature reclaiming the gravel path with tall grass and stubborn weeds. The fence line that had once neatly defined their land was broken in several places, likely by desperate people or wandering animals.

Their sprawling ranch house, once a symbol of safety and family, stood silent and neglected. Windows were shattered, probably from looters or storms that no one had been around to clean up after. Dark stains marred the walls.

It's been less than four months. How is everything falling apart so quickly? She examined the stains and brushed a finger against them, smearing a strange black goop. *What the hell is that? Whatever it was must have been in the air.*

The old oak tree where she had built a treehouse for Junior still stood, but the rope ladder hung in tatters, swaying gently in the breeze.

Oh, Junior, she lamented.

In the distance, where she should have been able to see the faint outline of Cedar Valley, there was only a hazy smudge on the horizon. Whether it was smoke from fires or just the distortion of heat waves, she couldn't tell.

The air was thick with unfamiliar scents. Gone were the comforting smells of freshly cut grass and Pa's barbecue. Instead, the wind carried the musty odor of decay and the sharp tang of something unnatural—perhaps the scent of the growlers themselves.

But it was the silence that struck Jennifer most profoundly. The constant background noise of rural life—the lowing of cattle, the distant bark of neighborhood dogs, the occasional passing car—had vanished. In its place was an oppressive quiet, broken only by the rustle of wind through overgrown grass and the occasional groan of a wandering growler.

Dozens of growlers were shambling aimlessly. They moved with eerie purpose yet seemed oblivious to her presence.

As her eyes swept across the sea of shambling figures, her heart clenched with a mixture of horror and recognition. There, near the old tractor, was Mr. Johnson from the feed store, his once-friendly face now a mask of vacant hunger. By the broken fence line, she spotted his twins, Emily and Erin, their matching outfits now tattered and stained with dark ichor. Then, with a jolt of pain, she saw Dennis, the boy from the supermarket who had smiled at her so warmly. Now, his eyes were white, and he stumbled in aimless circles. These weren't just anonymous monsters; they were the people she had grown up with, talked to, and laughed with. Now, they were trapped in a horrific limbo between life and death, their humanity stripped away.

A flash of movement caught her eye. Someone living, moving with purpose through the horde of growlers. As the figure drew closer, she felt her world tilt on its axis once more.

"Aunt Cass?" she said, her voice barely above a whisper.

Cassie was her older stepsister who everyone insisted Jennifer call Aunt Cassie, for reasons that Jennifer never understood. It was a strange custom but then Aunt Cass was a strange person. Jennifer had often visited her excentric sister. They had had the weirdest adventures together in underground places.

Cassie approached, looking utterly unfazed by the growlers around them. "Sorry it took me so long to get here," she said, her tone casual, as if she were apologizing for being late to a dinner party. "I thought you would be okay in your bunker. I did not account for those Billy brothers, though they were always real assholes. I sent this horde ahead to infect the Billy family."

Jennifer frowned. "You sent the horde?"

Nothing that Cassie said made sense to Jennifer. Cassie had always said strange things. She had been in and out of special hospitals because of the strange things she said and did. That was something she and Cassie had in common.

Jennifer felt tears welling up in her eyes, months of pent-up emotion threatening to overflow. "Ma, Pa, and Junior are dead," she choked out.

Cassie's attempt at a sad expression fell flat, looking more like a mild inconvenience. She let out a long breath. "It happens." She brought a small bottle out of her pocket. "What does this scent remind you of?" She sprayed the contents in Jennifer's face.

Jennifer's mind fogged for a moment. The scent reminded her of something, but she could not quite pin it down. She suddenly felt relaxed and at ease.

“Your perfume,” said Jennifer in a daze. “I always… loved it.”

Cassie's eyes softened slightly as she looked at her half-sister. "I’ve always had a special place in my heart for you, Jennifer. I was there when you were born. I saw you before our mother saw you. I'm going to take you somewhere safe, little sis," she said, reaching out to brush a strand of hair from Jennifer's face. "I have a lot to explain to you."

Cassie led her away from the bunker, away from the shambling horde that had once been her neighbors; Jennifer felt as if she were walking in a dream. The world as she had known it was gone, replaced by something unrecognizable and terrifying, but as she followed Cassie through the apocalyptic landscape, a small spark of hope flickered to life in her chest.

Whatever was happening, whatever Cassie had to explain, Jennifer knew one thing for certain: her life was about to change dramatically once again, and this time, she was determined to understand why.

9 months into the outbreak

The sprawling fields of Cassandra LaCroix's farm were a tranquil haven, seemingly untouched by the chaos that had engulfed the world. Rows of healthy crops swayed gently in the breeze, and livestock grazed contentedly in their pens.

In the weathered red barn, Cassandra, or "Cassie" as the locals knew her, knelt beside a newborn calf, gently coaxing it to drink from a bottle of milk.

Cassie, who was in her mid-thirties but looked younger, was a striking figure even in her work-worn clothes. Her ebony skin gleamed with a light sheen of perspiration, and her long black hair was intricately braided, practical yet beautiful. Her warm brown eyes sparkled with intelligence and compassion as she tended to the young animal.

"There you go, little one," she murmured, her voice soft and melodic. "That's it, drink up." As the calf suckled eagerly, Cassie smiled, a mixture of joy and sadness in her expression. "You know, you and I have something in common. We both lost our mothers too early."

She paused, running a gentle hand along the calf's flank. "But don't you worry. I'm here for you now." She chuckled softly and deftly checked the calf's vitals, her movements practiced and sure. "Your heartbeat is strong, your breathing is regular. You're doing just fine, sweetie."

From the barn door, Carter, Cassie's farm hand and protector, watched with an unreadable expression. His rugged features were softened by the hint of a smile, his bright red hair catching the sunlight streaming through the gaps in the barn's wooden slats.

"You're too soft on them, Miss Cassie," he said, his tone light but laced with a hint of frustration. "A year from now, you'll be finishing that one off and turning him into steaks. You and your father love your meat."

Cassie looked up, meeting Carter's gaze with a gentle but firm expression. "But first, it will have life, Carter, and that life should be nurtured with kindness. This little one will be part of a herd. A herd bred for a purpose. Living should be about kindness, about connection." She stood, wiping her hands on her tattered t-shirt. "Every creature on this farm, every person we meet, they all deserve compassion. It's what makes us human, what separates us from the horrors out there in the goings on."

She walked over to Carter, placing a hand on his arm. "Besides," she added with a mischievous glint in her eye, "happy cows make better steaks. It's science."

Carter couldn't help but laugh. "You always have an answer for everything, don't you?"

"Not everything," Cassie replied, her smile fading slightly. "But I do know that in this world, kindness is a strength, not a weakness. It's what will rebuild our communities, our world." She looked back at the calf, now sleeping peacefully. "Every life matters, Carter. Every moment of joy, every act of kindness...it all adds up."

Carter looked at her with a confused expression, which quickly changed to acceptance as he nodded. "Yes, ma'am."

She put a hand on his chest and slowly let it slide down to his groin. She squeezed his bulge and felt it react. She gently bit her lip. "We all have our purpose around here." She squeezed harder making him grimace, but he would not back away or move his hand to stop her. She took in a long deep breath and let it out slowly, watching his grimace grow wider.

A strangled gurgle bubbled up from Carter's throat.

She laughed, let go of him, turned and walked toward the front barn door. There was a bucket out of position by six inches; she frowned and slid it with her foot into its correct position.

Without warning, she turned and slapped Carter hard about the face. He stumbled back, putting a hand on his stinging cheek. He looked up fiercely at her for a brief moment and then his eyes fell to the floor.

"I'm sorry, ma'am, forgive me," he said hurriedly. "Not sure how that bucket got out of place."

She smiled benignly at him. "Bless your heart. Of course you're forgiven."

Still rubbing his cheek, he bowed. "Thank you, thank you, ma'am."

She turned away and walked toward the fields, looking back in time to see him roll his eyes and wander off via the side door, muttering something about taking a leak. She watched him go. A movement in her peripheral vision caught her eye. She looked out the barn to see a figure shambling up the long driveway.

She looked puzzled. "Someone is lost and needs some directions," she said to herself. She walked toward the figure with calm, confident strides. "Are you lost?" she asked softly. "You're not supposed to be up here."

The figure stopped its shambling gait and came to a sudden halt. Its head jerked. Its white eyes widened, and a black stream of liquid oozed from its mouth.

Cassie tilted her head in curiosity. "What's wrong?"

It growled and snarled.

"Don't be like that," she said and gently reached out her arm to its shoulder to guide it. "Come on, I'll show you the way. I know it's easy to get lost in those fields, isn't it."

The creature's eyes fixed on her face. It then allowed itself to be turned around.

"This way," she said calmly.

To anyone watching, it seemed like she was about to meet a gruesome end, but Cassie, with an air of serene authority, led the growler away from her property, her touch seemingly pacifying the creature. She guided it to the edge of her land and sent it off, watching it disappear into the distance.

Carter returned, his eyes wide with horror. "I'm sorry, ma'am," he stammered. "I just went to take a leak. I didn't think anything could happen."

Cassie turned to him, her expression softening into a smile. "Oh, I was fine, Carter." She glanced at her watch. She touched the screen of her watch. "I was safe."

Carter sighed with relief, but Cassie's gaze hardened. "But you did make a mistake abandoning your guard duties like that. I was never in danger; the real threat was toward you." She manipulated something on her watch.

"Please," Carter began, his voice trembling as his gaze fixed on her watch.

Cassie stepped closer, her hand reaching out to touch his groin. "I do like your meat," she said, her voice a silky whisper. "But that'll only get you so far."

Her watch beeped, and an anklet on Carter's leg responded in kind. His eyes went wide with shock, then turned a vacant, milky white. Cassie's expression twisted into a snarl. "You're no longer of use to me."

The anklet had injected a pure version of the virus directly into his bloodstream. Carter had been completely under her power, so the anklet device had not been a necessary threat, but Cassie installed it because she liked to see fear in her puppets.

She pointed in the same direction she had led the first growler. Carter turned and shambled away.

She watched him go, looking at his rear end. She made a wry smile. "Hmm, maybe I should have kept him around." She shook her head. One thing about men, they are all easily replaced."

"Peter!" she shouted. It was time to play with a new puppet.

A large, muscular man ran to her. "Yes, ma'am?"

"I think it's about time I dealt with these people who found a true vaccine for the Black. Pack my things. We'll leave after …" She paused and ran her hands over his large biceps. "Yes, we'll leave after."

Chapter

THE HERO'S BURDEN

Deacon - Paradise

Deacon wakes

Deacon's eyes snapped open, his heart racing as the echoes of growler snarls faded from his dreams. For a moment, disorientation gripped him as he stared at the unfamiliar ceiling of his new quarters in Paradise. The room was bathed in the soft, pre-dawn light filtering through makeshift curtains at the front of the shipping container, a far cry from the cramped, dark spaces they'd huddled in before the battle.

A month had passed since their desperate, against-all-odds victory, but the memories of that hellish battle still clung to him. He took a deep breath, grounding himself in the present, in the relative safety they'd carved out of the chaos.

Paradise, they called the community. Deacon couldn't help but wonder if they were tempting fate with such a name.

He yawned and sat on the edge of this bed, careful not to move his calves against the wooden pallets that served as his bed's foundation. His mattress and his blankets were made from various items of clothing. *It must be late if the sun is filtering in like that.*

The smell of his own stale sweat made him wrinkle his nose. They had rigged an old water tank on the roof, painted black to absorb heat from the sun. Copper pipes snaked down from the tank into his room, coiled to maximize heat absorption, and connected to a gravity-fed showerhead. The water was heated throughout the day by solar energy and stored in an insulated tank, enough for a few quick showers each morning and evening.

There was a spot near the entrance where he could shower. There was no privacy, but Deacon had decided not to complain as the community had higher priorities. *Modesty is second to survival.*

Eager to shake off the lingering unease from his dreams, he stripped and entered the shower. The warm water was a luxury he still hadn't gotten used to, and he closed his eyes, savoring the sensation as he rinsed.

His thoughts turned to Mary, as they often did when he showered. In his mind's eye he pictured her in the shower. *Wouldn't it be wonderful if we were just a few years older, and no one would bat an eye if…*

A soft giggle startled him from his reverie. His eyes flew open to find Mary standing there, her gaze unabashedly fixed on him, a mischievous smile playing on her lips. Mortification flooded through him as he scrambled to cover himself.

"Mary! What are you—you can't be here!" he sputtered, his face burning.

She leaned against the doorframe, staring at him unfazed. "Why not?"

Deacon's mind raced, imagining her father Sven's reaction if he caught them like this. "Your dad will kill me if he sees us," he hissed, fumbling for his towel.

Mary rolled her eyes, but her smile never wavered. "Dad needs to realize I'm not a little girl anymore. I am sixteen, and you're fourteen. In these times, that means we are adults."

"I'm fifteen," corrected Deacon.

Mary tilted her head to the side. "Fifteen?" She paused for a moment; her eyes widened. "You turned fifteen and didn't tell anyone?"

"It was just after the battle; I was in the hospital tent; there were dead bodies everywhere; what was I supposed to say? Stop burying those bodies and bake me a cake?"

Mary slowly nodded. "Yeah, that would have been…weird."

"Turn around so I can dress," he said.

She raised one defiant eyebrow, then smiled, shook her head, and began to turn around. Deacon dropped his towel and grabbed his clothes, but Mary turned all the way around so she was facing him again. She giggled as he frantically pulled on his underwear, getting them tangled for a moment but eventually covering himself. He looked at her with an accusatory expression.

She giggled again. "You said turn around, and I did. You didn't specify how many degrees of turning to do. You need to be specific."

A muscular bearded man walked past the shipping container, glanced at Mary and Deacon, frowned, and continued walking and muttering. Deacon recognized the man, Peter, who had voiced concerns about Deacon having some 'freaky' connection to the growlers.

As Deacon hastily dressed, acutely aware of Mary's unwavering gaze, he couldn't help but marvel at her confidence. It was so at odds with the nervous energy thrumming through his veins.

Maybe something's wrong with me. I should be more confident. I should sweep her off her feet and bed her right now, if that's what she really wants.

In haste, he caught the zip of his fly and tugged to free it. Mary strode forward. "Don't jerk it like that," she said, smiling broadly at her play on words. She batted his hands away from the zipper. She grabbed the zip and gently wiggled it. It loosened, and she lowered it. "See, you have to be gentle." She brought her face close to his.

Deacon felt warmth spreading over his face as he blushed deeply. *It isn't normal for a girl to be this forward, is it? Or is my understanding of girls all wrong.*

She knelt. "And now gently…slowly…up it goes." She pulled the zipper all the way up.

Oh, my lord, I am about to explode. Doesn't she know what she's doing to me? Of course she knows. Why am I even resisting her at this point? My one goal in life is to lose my virginity, and frankly, if her dad wants to kill me… Well, maybe it's just worth it.

Mary shook her head with a wry smile. "You know, for someone who saved an entire community, you're adorably shy."

It's okay for you, you're beautiful. You know everyone in their right mind would be attracted to you.

Deacon's cheeks burned hotter at her words, a mix of embarrassment and something else he couldn't quite name coursing through him. "What brings you to my hovel?"

Mary twirled a strand of her hair. "I just thought we would walk to breakfast together. It's venison sausages again."

Deacon nodded, his stomach growling at the mention of food. The community's decision to provide a daily communal breakfast had been a smart one. It ensured that even those who struggled with scavenging or hunting wouldn't starve, at least not completely. The gate tax—which was one tenth of any resources brought into Paradise—funded this shared meal, fostering a sense of unity and mutual support.

They left together and walked through the community. Deacon noted that Paradise's walls were now dotted with an array of salvaged speakers, which he knew were wired to a central control system, ready to broadcast Deacon's recordings of 'the voice'. The community had tested this system several times on small groups of passing growlers with remarkable success. Each time, Deacon's recorded command to "stand still" had frozen the creatures in their tracks, allowing for their swift and efficient disposal. This innovative defense mechanism had become a source of both security and pride for the residents of Paradise.

They walked toward the communal tent, and Deacon marveled at how quickly it had been constructed. Sheets of various colors and patterns had been haphazardly sewn together and suspended between shipping containers, creating a surprisingly large and airy space.

The path to breakfast gave Deacon a good view of Paradise's ongoing transformation. Everywhere he looked, people were hard at work. Some were reinforcing the perimeter defenses, while others were setting up more permanent living quarters or tending to the fledgling crops. The community buzzed with purposeful energy.

What struck Deacon most, however, was how people reacted to his presence. Conversations hushed as he passed, replaced by respectful nods or, from some of the younger residents, looks of barely concealed awe. There were a few looks of suspicion, even of disgust. Not everyone was comfortable with the idea that Deacon could listen to and command the growlers. An older man stepped aside to let them pass, offering a grateful smile that made Deacon's cheeks burn.

"Still not used to it, huh?" Mary whispered, noticing his discomfort.

Deacon shook his head. "I don't think I ever will be. A month ago, I was just...me. Now, it's like they expect me to have all the answers. I mean its… not like my idea was even that clever."

Mary giggled.

"You do that a lot," said Deacon.

Mary tilted her head. "Do what?"

Deacon looked at her with what he hoped was a friendly not condescending expression. "Giggle."

She smiled and rubbed her hand down his back. "Only around you," she said softly and then after a moment's pause, her hand squeezed his butt.

Deacon blushed, and then immediately hated himself for blushing… which made him blush more. He felt the burning sensation on his cheeks.

"Aw!" Mary squealed. "I love it when you blush. It's freaking adorable!"

Deacon shook his head with a smile. His cheeks were fire.

As they approached the communal tent, the smell of grilled meat made Deacon's mouth water, but even as his stomach rumbled in anticipation, he couldn't shake the weight of expectation that seemed to follow him everywhere in Paradise. People had called him a hero, a savior—titles he never asked for and believed were completely undeserved.

Inside they found Sven, the Professor, Samantha, Amanda, and Billy already seated at one of the long tables. Sven's eyes narrowed slightly as Mary slid onto the bench next to Deacon, but he said nothing.

Amanda, clipboard in hand, immediately zeroed in on Deacon. "Let me take a look at those wounds," she said, her tone leaving no room for argument.

As she examined the healing cuts and bruises, especially around his face, Deacon felt the weight of everyone's attention. He shifted uncomfortably, struggling to find the right words to express the doubts that had been plaguing him.

"They're healing nicely," Amanda declared, making a note on her clipboard. "How are you feeling otherwise, Deacon?"

He opened his mouth and closed it again, unsure how to respond. How could he admit to feeling lost, overwhelmed, and undeserving of their praise? His eyes flickered to Samantha, and suddenly, the words tumbled out.

"I'm not the hero everyone thinks I am," he said. "If people only knew how scared I was during the battle—"

"But you kept your wits about you," said Mary, rubbing his arm and then holding his hand, earning another look from her father.

Deacon shook his head. "People like Samantha are real heroes. The way she kept her wits about *her* when she was being interrogated in the bunker. Have you seen that video? Even with the president on a live feed, she didn't back down. She fought back, escaped, and brought down the cult's bunker...that takes real courage."

Samantha looked startled, then touched by his words.

The Professor looked lost in thought for a moment. "A live feed to the president…" he muttered, his eyes looking without focus. "That must have involved a satellite connection."

"I noticed they were adding more speakers on the wall," said Deacon and then bit into a sausage. "I think they should be adding more ditches…"

Billy shook his head. "Let the army figure out our defenses; they are the experts."

Deacon sighed in frustration. He didn't want the survival of the community to rely solely on his discovery of the voice. "But I don't think we should rely on the speakers."

"We're really not," said Billy. "We have an army battalion… Well, a third of a battalion… We have 97 professionally trained soldiers."

Sven grimaced. "We only have a 100,000 rounds. We used millions during the battle."

"We have RPGs," said Billy.

"Only 9 of them," said Sven

Billy's jaw tightened. "Well, that's why we're working on adding speakers."

"Speakers won't work if the cult attacks again," said Sven.

Billy banged his hand on the table. "The cult daren't show their face here. They've withdrawn from all the local communities."

Sven snorted. "It's called regrouping. They will be back and full of vengeance."

Deacon could see Billy's face turning red. "Everything has gotten better since the battle," said Billy. "Growler activity has decreased a lot; the cult has…gone away to regroup; we have planted more crops. Hunting has been … well, okay, hunting is getting harder because I guess we have hunted too much… and scavenging is getting harder…" Billy seemed to run out of enthusiasm.

Amanda put her hand on Billy's. "We've added extra physical defenses. We have deeper ditches and more of them *all* around the perimeter, they've all got spikes in them. We have new ramparts, and we've reorganized the whole community to have an orchestrated way of falling back into safety into redoubts. We have patrols out all the time looking for threats. Bert is out on patrol right now. The threat does seem to have receded. We make gun shops our number one priority whenever we venture into towns, so we'll get more ammunition for when the cult rears its ugly little head again."

"President Mitchel and his cult still control most of the army. Do you know how many rounds of ammunition the U.S. army has?" asked Sven.

No one answered for a while.

Deacon sighed. "A shit ton."

His comment elicited some sad laughter.

For the next few minutes, the conversation split into parallel discussions. Deacon found himself talking to the Professor about the virus.

"Explain to me one more time how a retrovirus works," he asked the Professor.

The professor grinned. Deacon knew he loved talking science. "Imagine a retrovirus as a tiny invader with a sneaky plan. First, it attaches itself to one of your cells and slips inside. But instead of just causing trouble right away, it has a clever trick up its sleeve—it carries a special tool that lets it rewrite its own instructions from a temporary form, like a sticky note we call RNA, into a permanent form, the DNA.

"Okay," said Deacon in a tone that said he was still unclear.

The professor continued, "The virus has its own program, which it sneaks into the control center of your cell like instruction in a book. Now, every time your cell reads that book, it unknowingly starts making copies of the virus. These new virus particles are then packaged up, break free from the cell, and go off to infect more cells, spreading the infection further."

"Yeah, but …" Deacon tried to interrupt, but the Professor was on a roll.

"Because the virus hides its instructions in the cell's book, it's really hard to get rid of, making it a particularly tough enemy."

"Yeah, but how does it make the infected behave like growlers?"

The Professor looked frustrated. "I've told you before. Much of our thinking is preprogrammed in our DNA. In a way, the virus just reprograms our behavior."

"So someone figured out how to reprogram people to be growlers?"

The Professor nodded.

"But why?" Deacon's voice cracked a little as he asked the question. He really wanted to understand what anyone had to gain by creating the outbreak.

"I really haven't a clue," said the Professor almost apologetically. "It's possible it's just the act of a crazy old man with more money than sense and with no morality."

"Someone with a lot of money? Like a billionaire?"

"Yes. They would need vast resources to make this work."

Deacon scratched his head for a moment. "I guess that's why he used the cult. They were in bed with the President, which means they had the whole infrastructure of the United States behind him."

The professor was silent for a moment. "Unfortunately, I think you're right. The man behind this, whatever his motives were, used the cult to carry out his plan."

The conversation continued for a while, meandering, touching on various community concerns, but no clear resolutions emerged. As the meal wound down, Deacon noticed Sven's gaze repeatedly flicking between him and Mary, a storm brewing behind his eyes.

"Deacon, Mary," Sven's gruff voice cut through the chatter as others began to disperse. "A word."

Deacon's stomach clenched. He exchanged a nervous glance with Mary as they remained seated.

Sven leaned in, his voice low but intense. "I've noticed you two getting...close." His eyes bored into Deacon. "These are dangerous times. Hormones running wild can lead to mistakes. Mistakes we can't afford."

Mary rolled her eyes. "Dad, we're not—"

"I'm not finished," Sven snapped. He took a deep breath, visibly reining in his temper. "I know you're both young, with urges." He took a deep breath and let it out slowly. He placed his hand on the table and slowly clenched it into a fist. "But you need to control your urges. For the good of the community and for Mary's safety and…" He looked Deacon in the eye. "…and for your safety."

Deacon squirmed in his seat, his face burning. "Sir, I would never—"

Sven's hand slammed down on the table, making them both jump. "Listen carefully, boy," he growled, his face inches from Deacon's. "Hero or not, if I catch you taking advantage of my daughter, I'll feed you to the growlers myself. Piece by piece. Understood?"

Deacon's mouth went dry, his heart pounding. He managed a weak nod, acutely aware of the threat behind Sven's words.

"Good." Sven straightened up, his demeanor shifting abruptly. He clapped Deacon on the shoulder, the gesture at odds with his previous menace. "Glad we had this talk. Now, off you go. Community needs you."

"Dad!" Mary said. "You're being very patronizing. I am not some stupid little girl. I am not a child. I can make my own decisions. If me and Deacon want to have sex, then we will."

Deacon gulped. He looked anxiously from Sven to Mary and mouthed, "Shut up!" to her.

Sven appeared to be considering her words. "Mary," he said calmly. He put his clenched fists on the table. "Fuck that! I will do what I must do to protect you. And you will do what you're told, or by God…" He closed his eyes and let out a long breath. He turned to Deacon. "I can't lay a finger on my little girl, I never have been able to find it in myself, but I sure as hell can lay a finger on you." He paused for a few seconds and placed a finger between Deacon's eyes. "You better go."

As they hurried away, Mary whispered, "I'm so sorry. He's just...protective."

Deacon nodded, unable to shake the chill of Sven's words. The man who had just threatened to dismember him was the same one who had fought beside him and bled with him. In this new world, it seemed, even allies could become enemies in the blink of an eye.

Phew! He was scary. Maybe I should try and keep my distance from Mary.

Mary walked in front of him, and his eyes fixed on her body. A wave of desire rushed through him with such ferocity he stumbled.

My God, what is wrong with me? In a world of growlers, the cult, the threat of starvation, of imminent death, here I am, pulled toward her like I am some kind of animal. Get a grip, Deacon!

Then a thought occurred. *My desire for her body, is that like the programmed behavior the Professor talked about. Somewhere in my DNA there is a message that makes me just lust after her with so much intensity I would die to* …He imagined their naked bodies hugging. *The growlers have been programmed to have an insatiable, irresistible desire to attack the living. It's the same kind of programming that is within me, just dialed up to infinity. If we could figure out how to turn off the growler instinct to kill, we could end this whole nightmare.*

"Oh look a dandelion," said Mary and bent over to pick it up.

Deacon felt another surge of lust as she bent over. *Unlike the growlers, I have control of my instincts. I want her so bad, but I hold back.*

She held the dandelion up to his lips. "Make a wish and make a big blow, if you get rid of all the seeds your wish will come true."

He smiled. *Sometimes she is like a child. I wish the growlers would all become human again.* He opened wide to blow, but she smooshed the dandelion into his mouth making him cough and choke.

"Ha! Ha!" she slapped her thigh and laughed. "I cant believe you fell for that."

Chapter

Billy, Amanda and Samantha

Billy - Paradise

Samantha – Billy - Amanda

Billy lay on his bed, partially sitting up, his eyes semi-open, in the dimly lit room. The dawn's first light filtered through a jury-rigged window in the container ceiling, casting a beam that danced with the dust in the air. Amanda's head rested on his chest, her golden hair splayed like a halo. Samantha was curled up on his other side, her arm draped over his bicep, breathing softly. The warmth of their bodies was a comforting reminder that even in this chaotic world, moments of peace and connection still existed.

He ran his hands through his hair and then gently pulled it before gritting his teeth and letting out a long hissing breath. His mind was far from peaceful. As head of the defense council, he carried the weight of the community's safety on his shoulders.

Here I am with two gorgeous women in my bed. Something I had never even dreamed of before the outbreak, but can I take a moment to enjoy it? No, all I can think about is growlers, the cult, raiders, and the politics of Paradise.

He shook his head gently not wanting to wake the two sleeping angels.

He had seen firsthand the horrors of the outside world: the relentless hordes of growlers, the viciousness of raiders, and the ever-present threat of scarcity. The community had fought hard to carve out this sanctuary, and it was his duty to protect it. The cult still cast a shadow over Paradise. Everyone knew they could return, set on vengeance.

He looked up at all the empty ammo boxes he was using to store his clothes, weapons, scant rations, and books.

Paradise spent nearly all its ammunition on the last battle. He had argued in the council to prioritize raiding for ammunition. There would be plenty of ammunition at Travis Airforce Base, which was a 10-hour hike away. He had planned a two-day operation to raid it, but he had been shot down in the high council. Food was their highest priority.

He had two granola bars in his food box, and a quarter bag of rice, and one can of tuna. Next to the food was his gun, which he knew had three bullets in, and he had no more. The community meals were going to get a lot leaner if more hunts came back empty.

Amanda, who led the health council, had argued for a raid on a hospital. The community's hospital tent had pitiful supplies remaining. "If there was another battle," Amanda had argued. "We'd be amputating with only aspirin for pain relief."

The community had mere days of food left, so reluctantly, both Amanda and Billy caved, and the only authorized raids were primarily for food.

Right now, we can't fend off a full-scale attack or even a medium-sized horde. If we go searching for ammo, we might starve. If we go searching for food, we are defenseless. If we have any outbreaks of illness or serious accidents, the hospital will look like a medieval torture chamber.

The battles they had fought to gain their freedom were etched in his memory, each loss a painful reminder of their fragility. But those battles had also forged a bond among the survivors, a sense of unity and purpose that was now the bedrock of their society. The defense council was a testament to that unity, a diverse group of individuals dedicated to the common goal of survival and prosperity.

Billy's thoughts drifted to the tasks that lay ahead. The perimeter defense that surrounded the community needed constant reinforcement. Patrols had to be organized, and scouts were sent out to gather intelligence on potential threats. The marketplace, bustling with traders and newcomers, was both a boon and a risk. It brought in much-needed resources and fostered a sense of normalcy, but it also meant strangers in their midst, each one a potential danger.

As he listened to the gentle breathing of Amanda and Samantha, he felt a surge of determination. He thought of the people who relied on him: the community members, traders, the children playing amid their ad hoc homes, the elders few thought they were.

They were his responsibility now, and he would do whatever it took to keep them safe.

He gently extricated himself from the embrace of the two women, careful not to wake them. He had patrols to coordinate. There was always work to be done, but for a brief moment, he allowed himself to appreciate the quiet, the love, and the fragile peace that they had built together.

Chapter

THE PATROL

Bert – Near the Sacramento River

Cassie running from growlers

The mid-morning sun beat down on Bert's neck as he trudged alongside the patrol. Sixty pairs of boots kicked up dust from the parched earth, a mix of seasoned soldiers and civilian volunteers. The Sacramento River glimmered in the distance, a silvery ribbon cutting through the landscape.

Ahead of him, on a high branch, there sat a solitary bird with a long neck and beak. *Whoa! That's a big egret. At times like this, I wish I were a bird. Imagine being able to beat your wings and escape whenever a growler showed up. Then again…imagine if the growlers could fly.* He shuddered at the thought of growlers descending from the skies. *Still, it would be nice to fly. I wonder if they marvel over the view. There again, I'm scared of heights. I wonder if there are birds that are scared of heights.* He chuckled at the thought of a bird that was scared of heights.

"Water break," Captain Reeves called out, his voice carrying over the rhythmic march.

Bert wiped the sweat from his brow, squinting against the cloudless blue sky. The heat was building, promising another scorcher of a day. He was about to take a swig from his canteen when a figure burst from the trees ahead.

"Help! Please, help me!" A middle-aged Black woman stumbled toward them, her clothes torn and face etched with terror.

The patrol snapped to attention, weapons raised. Captain Reeves approached cautiously. "Ma'am, identify yourself!"

"Cassie," she gasped, bent over and panting. "There are growlers...chasing me..."

Bert's heart started racing. He was glad he had cleaned his gun and fully loaded all his magazines before heading out with the patrol. He chambered a round and flipped off the safety.

Reeves barked orders, and the patrol formed a defensive perimeter. "How many? Which direction?"

Cassie shook her head, still struggling to catch her breath. "I don't know...at least a thousand. They're minutes behind me."

"Shit," Bert muttered, tightening his grip on his rifle. *A thousand could easily overwhelm us.*

Captain Reeves pointed at Chuck, a volunteer who carried a Bluetooth speaker and a smartphone with a recording of the meta mind's voice, giving the order that would make the growlers stop. "Play the damn thing, Chuck!"

A guttural growl pierced the air, sending chills down Bert's spine. The trees erupted with movement, a seething mass of rotting flesh and snapping jaws sprinting forth.

"Open fire!" Reeves roared, his voice barely audible over the sudden cacophony of snarls and moans.

The air exploded with gunfire, muzzles spurting fire amid the grim faces of the patrol. Bert's world narrowed to the sights of his rifle. The army trainer had warned him of the dangers of firing without thinking or aiming. Ammunition was limited. The trainer had lectured the volunteers, "It's way too easy to spray bullets in the air and hit nothing. In a firefight, it's not who fires the most; it's who scores the most hits."

Bert was trying to make every shot count, but the growlers were getting close, and his fear was rising to the point of panic. He remembered more of the trainer's words, "With growlers, there's no such thing as suppressive fire. Growlers never seek cover. Growlers cannot be pinned down. They just sprint at you."

He exhaled slowly, squeezing the trigger. The first growler's head exploded in a spray of black gore. Another shot, another fallen creature. But for everyone that dropped, two more seemed to take its place.

"Conserve ammo!" Reeves bellowed. "Headshots only! Make every round count! Chuck, play the damn thing."

Bert tried to steady his breathing, aiming carefully. A growler with half its face missing charged at him jaws gnashing. He waited until the last second, then fired. The creature collapsed at his feet, twitching.

The recording started to play its eerie sound, which was hard to hear amid the growls, snarls, yells, and gunfire.

To his left, a civilian volunteer screamed as a growler latched onto his arm. Before Bert could react, one of the soldiers pivoted, firing a three-round burst that demolished the growler's skull. The civilian stumbled back, clutching his bleeding arm.

Some of the growlers seemed to hesitate.

Shit! The speakers aren't loud enough. There's too much noise for them to hear our meta-mind voice.

Bert watched in horror as Corporal Ramirez, the patrol's combat medic, spotted the injured civilian stumbling, holding his bitten arm. Without hesitation, Ramirez sprinted toward him while gunfire streamed all around.

"I got you!" Ramirez shouted, dragging the injured man to the ground as the sounds of inhuman snarls filled the air.

Bert knew what needed to be done to stop the man from turning.

"This is morphine; hang in there," Ramirez said, prepping the autoinjector. He plunged it into Jenkins' thigh, the man's body relaxing slightly as the painkiller took immediate effect.

Ramirez pulled a tourniquet from his med kit, wrapping it tightly around the upper arm. "This is gonna hurt like hell, but it might save your life," he muttered, cranking the windlass until the blood flow ceased.

A growler suddenly lunged forward, jaws snapping. Bert rapidly put two rounds through its eye socket without missing a beat. Black blood sprayed out, and the growler collapsed.

Ramirez reached into his pack, pulling out a battery-powered saw. Its diamond-edged circular blade whirred to life with a high-pitched whine. Amanda said the circular saw was not exactly a medically sound way of amputating limbs, but their options were limited, and she envisioned the need for rapid amputations on the battlefield.

The man looked at the saw and then at Ramirez. "Holy shit, no way."

The medic took a deep breath, steadying his hands. In one swift motion, he brought the blade down on the arm, just below the tourniquet. The device cut through flesh, muscle, and bone within five seconds. The man's scream rose above the raucous sound of the growlers.

Blood spurted, but Ramirez was ready. He clamped the major blood vessels and then applied a hemostatic agent to the wound. Ramirez reached into his bag again, removing a pen-like device. Bert watched him apply it to the wound and heard a sizzling sound.

Seconds later, Ramirez had the stump wrapped in sterile bandages.

Bert had continued to provide cover for the medi. He had to reload several times. He noticed the severed arm on the ground, twitching. Part of him wondered if that was natural or related to infection.

The speaker isn't working.

The growlers were still emerging from the woods. There did not seem to be an end to the onslaught. Some of the nearby growlers were moving slowly, others were continuing to charge. There was something about the pattern of their attack that looked odd. He couldn't quite figure it out, but something was weird.

"We're burning through ammo too fast," someone shouted over the din.

Bert looked down at the magazines on his jacket. Half were empty. *Shit!* He had even dropped one of the magazines during a reload and had to retreat, leaving it behind. His stomach knotted as he realized they were being overwhelmed.

"Form a circle!" Reeves commanded. "Back to back! Don't let them flank us!"

Talk English captain, thought Bert, *what does flanking even mean. We're civilians; we don't understand military jargon.*

The patrol scrambled to obey, forming a tight ring. Bert found himself shoulder to shoulder with a young soldier, both of them firing in controlled bursts at the encroaching horde.

Then he saw it—a massive growler, easily seven feet tall, barreling through its smaller brethren. It charged straight for the captain.

"Big one! Eleven o'clock!" Bert shouted, but it was too late.

The behemoth growler crashed into the captain, burying its teeth into his neck, then arching back, ripping flesh and tendons.

Panic rippled through the patrol. Their leader was gone.

"Fall back!" a corporal ordered. "Leapfrog retreat! Odd numbers cover; even numbers move!"

Bert had thought they were leaderless, but the army knew what to do; the army had a chain of command that they all understood.

The trainer had taught the volunteers about doing a leapfrog retreat. "Those with odd numbers stay in position, laying down fire to keep the enemy at bay, while the even-numbered troops swiftly move fifty strides back. Once there, they would return fire, allowing the odd-numbered soldiers to retreat in turn."

They had all been assigned numbers, but in the heat of battle, Bert suddenly could not remember what his number had been. He decided to be an odd number, so he stood his ground, firing steadily as half the patrol retreated.

His rifle clicked empty. He dropped the spent magazine, hands shaking as he reached for a fresh one. *I only have three magazines left.*

In that split second of vulnerability, a growler lunged at him. Bert stumbled backward, his foot catching on a fallen log. He crashed to the ground, feeling a sharp pain as a branch scraped his ankle.

He rammed the magazine in place, but it was too late. Just as the growler launched itself on him, he put his feet between himself and it. Rotting hands clawed at him, tearing at his trouser leg. Bert kicked up frantically, his boot connecting with decaying flesh, but the creature held on, its teeth snapping.

A blade flashed in the sunlight. The growler went limp, a knife buried to the hilt in its skull. Cassie stood over him, her face spattered with black blood, eyes wild.

"Thanks," Bert gasped as she hauled him to his feet.

"Don't thank me yet," Cassie growled, yanking her knife free with a sickening squelch. "Look!"

Bert turned to see the massive growler that had killed the captain, and now it was bearing down on them, a macabre trail of broken bodies in its wake. Its milky eyes seemed to focus on them with terrifying intelligence.

“Odds retreat!” shouted the corporal.

"Run!" Bert yelled, grabbing Cassie's arm.

They sprinted toward the retreating patrol, the thunderous footsteps of the behemoth growler shaking the ground behind them. Bert's ankle screamed in protest with each step.

A stream of bullets ripped into the growler's chest, but it continued forward until one bullet took the side of its head off.

When Bert looked back, the giant growler was down, but incredibly, it was still moving, dragging itself forward with single-minded determination until another bullet exploded what was left of its brain.

The gunfire was tapering off, the immediate threat neutralized. Only crawling-disabled growlers remained. But when Bert met Cassie's eyes, he saw only fear.

Some of the growlers had stopped and even began to walk away.

Finally, the voice recording is working.

"There's more coming," Cassie said, her voice hoarse. "A lot more."

The corporal who was now in command was already on the radio, his words clipped and urgent. "Paradise, this is Patrol Seven. We've engaged a group of growlers, approximately 200 strong. Heavy casualties. Intel suggests a larger force inbound. Prepare for imminent attack. We're falling back now."

That was only 200; it certainly felt like the thousand Cassie had described.

As they began their hasty retreat, Bert limped alongside Cassie, his mind reeling from the close call. "That was some knife work back there," he said, trying to mask his adrenalin-fueled shakiness with casual conversation.

Cassie's only response was a grim nod. Her eyes quickly glancing back, she was no doubt scanning for the next wave of horror that awaited them.

Her face was expressionless, as if the last year of survival had caused every emotion to be exhausted or suppressed. "When you've been out here as long as I have, you learn a few tricks."

She's grown strong…or maybe she always was strong. Oh, if I were only thirty years younger, a nice black girl like this would have been… He smiled as he remembered past lovers before tragedy had moved his life off track.

His leg was throbbing. Every step felt like it was making it worse. He knew he had to ignore the pain. *If there are thousands of growlers behind us, I can't slow the patrol down. We have to get to Paradise and prepare for the attack.* He looked down at his leg; it was already swelling and was covered in blood. It looked like the branch had scraped a large part of his lower leg and ankle.

Cassie was running in front of him. He looked at her and grinned. *Damn, she's fine.*

The pain in his leg and his bursting lungs made him shake his head.

I am too damn old for this.

Chapter

THE FAILED DEFENSE

Billy - Paradise

Injured Bert

Billy was digging a ditch with Deacon by his side when the crackle of the speaker system indicated that Command was about to speak. The new ditch was immediately in front of the container wall and was intended to make it hard for growlers to form ladders over the wall.

"Stand to! Stand to! Patrol is coming in hot!" the speakers announced. "Stand to! Stand to! Patrol is coming in hot!"

Billy felt his heart start thumping hard and fast. "Deacon, you head to Command and prepare the voice, do a test. We cannot afford some technical snafu."

I know they can do it without him, but I'd rather see him safe up in the Command tower.

"Yes, sir." Deacon immediately tried to climb out of the ditch but stumbled over some unplanted spikes.

Billy caught him. "Jesus! Careful kid. This is no time to impale yourself."

"No, sir," said Deacon and ran off toward the gates.

A movement in the trees caught Billy's attention. The patrol emerged, heading down the path to the front gate; as they passed each ditch, they removed the planks that acted as bridges.

Jesus, it must be a big horde; they look rattled.

An all-too-familiar sound filled the air. It was the sound of a mass of growlers, all howling and snarling and pounding their feet as they sprinted toward the community.

Billy raced to the gates and saw Amanda waiting inside to triage the patrol. One of the patrol members was missing an arm, another had a gash on the side of his face, and Bert was limping, trailing blood behind him.

They must have had one hell of a battle.

As soon as the patrol was safely in the community, Amanda focused set about triaging her patients.

"Prepare to close the gates!" shouted Billy. He knew he had to give time for people who were working on the ditches to get inside.

Gunfire erupted which Billy knew meant that the growlers had reached the outer ditches. It was unclear how big the horde was as it was still emerging from the forest.

Billy knew the ditches would not stop the growlers; they were only intended to slow them down so the guns could do their job.

The real defense would be the use of the voice from all the speakers on the walls.

"Hurry up inside!" Billy shouted.

The gates consisted of two trucks, each carrying a shipping container and a thick steel plate welded onto the side. On top, there were ramparts. One truck was the outer gate, and the other was the inner gate. The trucks needed to pull forward to completely block the entrance.

The sound of the growls was getting louder. The gunfire from atop the containers increased.

We can't afford to expend so much ammunition. We should hold fire and let the speakers do their work.

The last few stragglers ran inside, and Billy waved at the trucks to close the entrance.

Billy approached Amanda to see if she needed help. Only then did he see the big slash in Bert's leg, ankle, and foot.

"Ouch," he said in sympathy.

"It looks worse than it is," said Bert with a grimace. "Tore it on a fallen branch."

Billy knelt and put his hand on Bert's shoulder. "Amanda will get you fixed up; I have to get to the ramparts and help."

Peter Sinly happened to be nearby. He stroked his beard, bent down to examine the wound, and shook his head. "That's a bite," he said in a low voice, then straightened up. We've got a bite here," he said in a louder voice.

"It's not a bite," said Bert.

"I know a bite when I see one," said Peter, removing his gun from his shoulder and charging it.

"Whoa! Whoa!" said Billy.

"It wasn't a bite," said Bert. "It was a branch."

Peter pointed his gun at Bert.

A woman stepped in front of Bert, blocking the shot. "I was there; he fell over a branch while protecting me. I saw it."

"Cassie…" Bert started, gesturing for her to step out of the way.

"No, it's true. The patrol saved me." Cassie stared at Peter defiantly.

Who is this woman? thought Billy. *I like her style.*

Amanda knelt and inspected the wound closely. "Were there any growlers nearby?"

Bert was silent for a moment, then nodded.

"Can you tell the difference between a scrape from a stick and a bite?" asked Billy.

Amanda shook her head. "This wound could be caused by either. The way growlers tear flesh and the way a jagged stick would tear flesh. It's impossible to be sure."

Peter pushed Cassie aside with the butt of his gun.

"Wait!" shouted Amanda, putting her hand up. "We have protocols for this. He gets handcuffed to a hospital cot." She looked at Billy. "Give me a hand. You can help out at the ramparts afterward."

Billy nodded, and he took Bert under his shoulders while Amanda and Cassie took his feet. They rushed him toward the hospital.

The community speaker system crackled to life. *"Oh, good. Deacon is going to use the voice. We've used up too much ammunition already." The speakers emitted the strange snarling,* growling recording of the voice that had halted and pacified the horde in the last battle.

They got to the hospital bed and quickly handcuffed Bert to a cot.

"Sorry, bud," said Billy. "It's just the protocol. In an hour, if you're not running a fever, we'll be able to uncuff you."

Bert grimaced and then grinned. "No problem. Now go finish off that horde."

Billy knew that once the horde stopped charging the walls, the growlers would just stand there and allow themselves to be killed. Deacon's little trick was a miracle that had saved them when all seemed lost.

He ran to the front ramparts, but before he even arrived, he knew something was wrong. The voice should have worked by now, but the gunfire was still rapid. He sprinted to a ladder and climbed up onto the community walls.

The first thing he noticed was how half the ammo boxes were empty. The horde were still attacking.

"Make every round count!" he shouted.

"Duh," said a soldier, carefully squeezing off a few well-aimed rounds.

He saw the Deacon at the front of the container staring at the horde. He was holding a device pointed at the crowd.

"Is it a technical problem? Is the voice not loud or clear enough?" asked Billy.

Deacon shook his head. "No technical problem; they're just not obeying the voice anymore. They have a new voice." He held up a hand and then made a hush signal. "I am recording the new voice."

A new voice. What the hell does that mean? Does Deacon understand what's going on? He was tempted to ask questions, but Deacon looked like he was concentrating. *I better not interrupt.*

Billy watched a new ammo box get opened. He looked down at the horde. They had reached the inner perimeter wall and were beginning to form ladders out of their own bodies. At first, the ditches against the wall appeared to be working. A few growler ladders fell down quickly, but they adapted, and soon, the structures began to rise up the walls.

He saw a corporal nearby. Billy turned to him. "We need to use RPGs on those ladders, break up the clumps of growlers." The problem with growler ladders was that even if you headshot the growlers, they stayed linked together. A grenade might blow the limbs apart, making it fall.

The corporal hesitated as the growler ladder grew to over half the height of the wall. He nodded and turned to his men. "You, you, and you. RPGs on those growler ladders now."

Once given their orders, the soldiers responded rapidly and efficiently. Within seconds, they had put several RPG rounds into the three growler ladders, which was enough to destroy them.

That was the last of the RPGs. Now what?

Deacon was wearing headphones now, listening intently to something. The growls and howls suddenly changed to murmurs. The horde has become still. Billy watched as their heads tilted.

Finally, the voice is working.

A cheer went up from the ramparts.

"Alright," said the corporal. "Now we can take our time. One bullet per growler from here on."

The remaining growlers began to walk away.

Billy "Whoa! Why are they walking away? That's not what the voice tells them to do. Last time, they just stood still and let themselves be killed."

The corporal put his hand on Billy's shoulder. "Just be grateful that Deacon's voice trick worked; we are almost out of ammunition. We urgently have to raid and get replenished."

Deacon was staring at the retreating growlers.

"You did it," said Billy. "Saved the day again."

Deacon shook his head. "It wasn't the voice I recorded. There's another voice. It told them to head to…" His eyes lost focus for a moment. "South, to Alameda naval base."

"You heard the voice say that?" asked the corporal.

"Not so much heard…" Deacon shook his head. "It's like I felt it."

Felt it? Billy didn't like the sound of that. Some people in the community were a little suspicious of Deacon for being able to hear the voice of the meta mind when others could not. *What would they think if he could feel the growler's meta mind?*

Billy watched the corporal assess Deacon with an expression of suspicion.

"The growlers are evolving," said Billy. "It's a damn good job we have Deacon to help us anticipate and adapt."

Deacon started to walk away, muttering to himself.

Shit, kid, don't look crazy. Billy touched his shoulder. "Where are you going, Deacon?"

"I need to analyze this new voice, perhaps get the Professor's opinion on it," he responded.

Billy nodded. "Good idea."

If shit gets weirder, we'll need to know what to expect.

Chapter

THE PUPPET MASTER

Cassie - Paradise

Cassie beckons one of her puppets.

There was a soft creaking of metal as the door to the shipping container swung open. Cassie emerged, her face a mask of calm composure, belying the cunning machinations whirring in her mind. Peter and a handful of her loyal followers stood guard, their eyes darting nervously into the shadows.

Cassie's gaze settled on Peter, a flicker of amusement dancing in her eyes. "Hide the radio again," she murmured, her voice low and conspiratorial. "We can't have anyone stumbling upon our little secret."

Her mind flashed back to a moment years ago, a moment that had been the first real test of her 'little trick,' as she had come to call it.

She had been at a restaurant with Jennifer, celebrating her little sister's birthday. The waiter, a young Peter, had been clumsy and inattentive, spilling drinks and mixing up their orders.

Cassie had watched him with a calculating eye, her hand toying with a small vial in her pocket. Inside was a perfume she had created, one laced with a potent retrovirus designed to deliver targeted DNA-based behavioral training.

When Peter had leaned over to clear their plates, Cassie had seized her chance. She sprayed the perfume directly into his face, a quick, discreet burst that went unnoticed by the other diners.

The effect had been immediate and startling. Peter's eyes had glazed over, his expression going slack. Then, as if a switch had been flipped, his whole attitude changed; he had snapped to attention, his gaze fixated on Cassie with an intensity that bordered on worship.

"Can I do anything for you, anything at all?" he had asked, his voice trembling with eagerness.

Cassie had smiled a slow, predatory grin. “It worked!” she had said to Jennifer. “I’ve tried it on hundreds of people without success, but it worked on this one.” She turned back to Peter. "For starters, you can comp our meal. And then, I have some other tasks for you."

From that moment on, Peter had been her loyal servant, the first of many who would fall under her sway.

Her thoughts came back to the present.

Peter slipped the radio back into its concealed compartment. The others shifted uneasily, their eyes betraying their curiosity, but they knew better than to question their leader.

Cassie surveyed her small group, a smile playing at the corners of her lips. "Everything is proceeding exactly as planned," she purred, her voice filled with self-satisfaction. "The horde, the patrol, even poor, deluded Bert—all dancing to my tune."

She laughed then, a cold, mirthless sound all too familiar to her followers. "Men are so predictable." She sneered, her eyes glittering with malice. "Flash a bit of vulnerability, play the damsel in distress, and they'll fall over themselves to be the hero. It doesn't hurt that I have a nice ass. Bert never stood a chance."

The others exchanged glances, unsure whether to join in her mirth or remain silent. Cassie paid them no mind, her thoughts already racing ahead to the next phase of her grand design.

"We will soon end this little vaccine production here in Paradise," she declared, her tone brooking no argument. "Then, we make our move on the bunker with the lab, the research, the specimens, and its other little treasures."

She paused, her gaze sweeping over her followers once more. "But first," she murmured, her voice taking on a husky, seductive edge, "I have other needs that require attention."

Her eyes locked with Peter's. Cassie crooked a finger, beckoning him closer, a wicked smile playing on her lips.

"Service me," she commanded, her voice a silky purr. "I need to be properly satisfied before I go back to playing the victim. You know the kind of work I need done on me."

Peter swallowed hard, nodded, and stepped forward to obey. The others averted their eyes, knowing better than to show any reaction.

Cassie led Peter back inside the container. For thirty minutes, the followers stayed outside and listened to her groans, the sound of leather hitting flesh, and her barely contained screams. Finally, Cassie gave a series of shuddering gasps.

She and Peter emerged. Peter's eyes were downcast, but Cassie had complete composure. She met each of her followers' eyes and grinned. She straightened her clothing, a cruel smile playing on her lips.

"Back to work, my little puppets," she crooned, her voice filled with dark promise. "We have mischief to get done."

Her followers scattered to their assigned tasks. Cassie slipped back into the shadows, ready to resume her role as the innocent survivor.

Peter was left by his container. He had tears in his eyes, a look of shame on his face, and blood seeping from his ear.

Chapter

Bert Restrained

Bert - Paradise

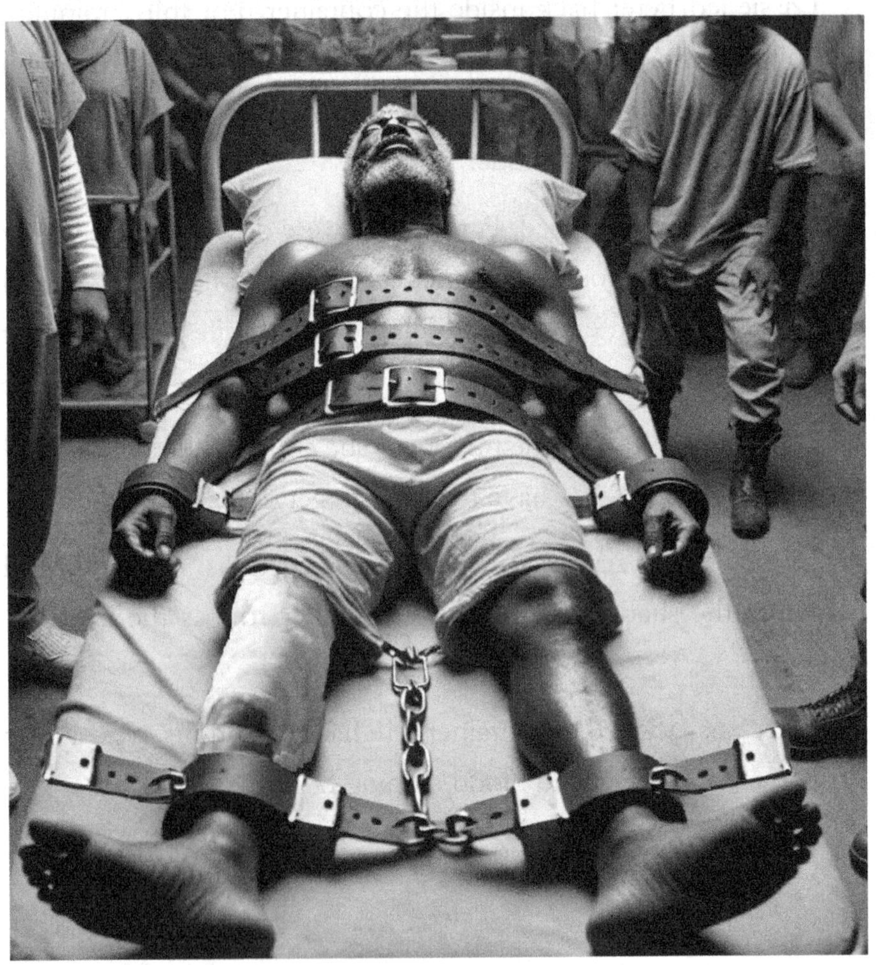

Bert Strapped Down

The metal and leather of the handcuffs bit into Bert's wrists as he shifted uncomfortably on the cot. Every movement sent a fresh wave of pain through his injured foot, making him wince. Amanda's gentle hands worked methodically, cleaning the wound with practiced efficiency.

"How's it looking, doc?" Bert asked, trying to keep his voice light despite the pain and worry gnawing at him.

Amanda glanced up, offering a reassuring smile. "I'm a nurse, not a doc. It's a nasty gash, but you're going to be okay, Bert. We've seen worse, haven't we?"

He nodded, remembering some of the gruesome injuries they'd treated since the outbreak began. The sharp sting of alcohol on his wound brought him back to the present with a hiss.

"Sorry," Amanda said, not pausing in her work. "Our medical supplies are running low, so we're using the community still's finest moonshine as antiseptic. Might not smell so good, but it'll do the job."

Bert chuckled, then grimaced as another bolt of pain shot through his foot. "Well, at least if I'm stuck here, I could use a drink of that stuff. Just uncuff me so I can sit up."

Amanda shook her head, but he caught the hint of amusement in her eyes. "You know the protocol, Bert. Twenty-four hours observation, cuffed for everyone's safety. If you don't develop a fever, you'll be free to go."

The pain is getting worse. I suppose my adrenaline has worn off.

As she finished bandaging his foot, Bert became acutely aware of a warmth spreading through his body. At first, he dismissed it as a reaction to the alcohol or maybe just the stress of the situation. But as the heat intensified, a cold dread settled in his stomach. He could feel sweat beading on his brow.

"Amanda," he said, his voice suddenly hoarse. "I think...I think I'm feeling hot."

Amanda's head snapped up, her eyes widening slightly before she schooled her features into a calm expression. "Let's not jump to conclusions. It could be a normal reaction to the injury and treatment. I'll check your temperature, okay?"

She moved to get the thermometer; Bert closed his eyes, trying to will away the heat he felt building inside him. *This is just my imagination.* He thought of all the people he'd come to care for in Paradise, of the life they were trying to build. *Please*, he thought, *let this just be a normal fever.* The alternative was too horrifying to contemplate.

Bert lay, waiting for Amanda to return with the thermometer; his mind wandered back to the chaotic moments of the ambush. The gunfire, the snarls of the growlers, the acrid smell of decay...it all came rushing back in vivid detail.

He remembered stumbling, falling backward, and then...Bert's breath caught in his throat as the memory crystallized. There had been a growler on his legs, its rotting hands clawing at him. He had kicked it off, but in that frantic moment, had he felt teeth break skin? The uncertainty gnawed at him, worse than any physical pain.

If I had thought it was a bite, I would have said something. They could have amputated. It's not a bite. It's definitely not a bite. This is me being a hypochondriac.

Amanda returned, thermometer in hand. Before she could take his temperature, Bert blurted out, "Amanda, I just remembered. There was a growler on me during the ambush. On my legs. What if...what if I was actually bit?"

Amanda's hand paused, hovering over his forehead. She met his gaze, her expression a mix of concern and professional calm. "Bert, let's not get ahead of ourselves. We'll check your temperature and go from there."

She placed the thermometer in his mouth, and Bert mumbled around it, "But I feel hot. Really hot. Could it be an infection already?"

Amanda shook her head slightly. "It's unlikely for an infection to cause a fever this quickly, Bert. Try to stay calm while we get an accurate reading."

The moments ticked by with tense silence. Bert could hear the rustle of movement around them, whispered conversations just out of earshot. He noticed a few people glancing nervously in his direction.

When she finally removed the thermometer, her brow furrowed as she read it. She didn't say anything, but her silence spoke volumes.

"What is it?" Bert asked, his voice barely above a whisper.

Before Amanda could respond, there was a flurry of activity in the hospital tent. Bert watched as other patients were hurriedly moved away from his cot, their faces a mix of fear and pity. The realization of what was happening hit him like a physical blow.

"Amanda," he said, his voice cracking. "Tell me the truth. Am I...am I turning?"

The look in Amanda's eyes told him everything he needed to know, even before she could find the words to respond.

“I'm so sorry, Bert,” she put her hand on his shoulder.

Jesus, help me. It was a bite, and it's too late to amputate. He pictured himself as a growler. *God, don't let me hurt my friends.* He knew what they would do when he turned. *A bullet to the head. I wonder who will do it.*

A deep, pervasive ache began to spread through his body, seeping into every muscle and joint. *Gawd! This is moving quickly.* As the pain intensified, his mind drifted, memories flooding in like a tide.

He saw his mother's kind face, weathered by years of hard work but always ready with a smile. His father's calloused hands, strong and steady as they taught him to fix an engine. The sweet scent of his wife's perfume as they danced at their wedding, full of hope for the future.

Then, darker memories surfaced: the cold concrete of Oakland's streets, where he'd slept after losing everything, the gnawing hunger, the crushing loneliness. Even those memories held a bittersweet quality now, knowing they had led him here, to Paradise, to this makeshift family he'd found amidst the apocalypse.

Family: I always wanted a family. Lord, in your wisdom, you took ... his thought was interrupted by a searing pain that jolted up his spine and into his head. His temples felt like nails were being hammered into them.

Amanda's cool hand on his forehead brought him back to the present. She was placing a cold compress on his brow, her eyes full of sorrow and determination.

The coolness immediately helped with the pain.

"Bert," she said softly, "I'm so sorry, but...there is no doubt now that you were bitten. Your fever is rising rapidly, and we need to take precautions." She paused, swallowing hard. "We're going to need to put in a gag for everyone's safety. I'm so, so sorry." She turned to a young girl who was helping her. "Can you get the gag, please?" The girl nodded and scurried away.

Bert wanted to protest, to say it wasn't necessary, but he knew it was necessary. He just nodded, closing his eyes as tears began to form. *This is happening; I am going to become one of those … things, and my friends are going to have to put a bullet in my brain and then burn me.*

"You are family to us, Bert," Amanda whispered, squeezing his hand. "We're going to be right here with you, okay?"

Family, yes, family.

Deacon entered the tent and rushed over to him. "Bert! I heard—" He came to an abrupt halt. His eyes widened. "Bert!" He flung his arms around him and hugged him.

Oh, that feels good. Family. But what if I suddenly turn? What if I bite him? I would never. I would never.

He shook his head at the boy. "You've got to keep your distance, kid."

Deacon looked at Amanda, his eyes asking a question and also pleading for that question not to be answered. She just nodded. Deacon's mouth dropped open and then closed. His lips quivered for a moment. "No! It's not fair!" he shouted.

Bert watched tears stream onto the boy's cheeks. *He really does care. What did I do to deserve a place in his heart?*

Amanda brought up a chair and gestured for Deacon to sit. Bert noticed she kept positioning the chair so Deacon would be out of biting range. She rubbed the boy's shoulder. "If you want to talk, do it now. When the gag goes in, he won't be able to answer."

Bert watched the boy struggle to manage his emotions. The boy's lips quivered, and he took two halting breaths. "Why?" the boy croaked.

"It's God's will," said Bert.

Deacon's fists clenched, and he bit his lip and then shook his head. "Why would God allow this? How can you believe in a God that has allowed so much suffering?"

"We cannot know God's plan," said Bert.

"No, no, no, NO!" said Deacon, spitting his words. "If God is good, and if God is all-powerful, then how can he allow this... how can he allow any of this to happen? It doesn't make sense. Either God is not all-powerful, or he is not good, which means that he isn't God. God cannot exist if all this suffering exists." There was venom in his tone and tears in his eyes.

Existence is hard enough with God, let alone without Him.

"Listen, Deacon," Bert looked over at the boy. His heart ached for him. "How do I explain this... Listen. If a human kills a child, you know that human is bad, right?"

Deacon looked puzzled. "Yes, you should never harm a child. That is a bad person."

Bert took in a deep, painful breath. He felt his lungs aching. "If a lion happened to come across a child and ate it, then is that a bad lion?"

Deacon was quiet for a moment and then shook his head. "No, a lion is just doing what is in its nature. It can't really be blamed."

"Exactly," said Bert. "We judge a lion differently than a human because it has a different nature, and we understand that, but let me ask you: do you understand the nature of God?"

"How can anyone understand the nature of God?" said Deacon.

Bert smiled. "There you have it, son. You cannot judge God. Our minds cannot grasp something infinitely good, infinitely powerful. Something that exists outside of time. So, don't let the suffering push you away from God; instead, make it a time where you seek His embrace."

Deacon stared back, his eyes filled with water.

Bert coughed. He saw a fine spray of Black come out of his mouth, and then a searing pain wracked his chest. He groaned.

"Try to rest, Bert," said Amanda.

He wanted to say something comforting, something significant, something profound before they put the gag in. The pain in his temples returned, and he felt the world begin to fade around him, Amanda's voice growing distant. He tried to hold onto consciousness, but it slipped away like water through his fingers.

When he came to, the first thing he noticed was the gag in his mouth, firm and unyielding. He tried to move, only to find his arms, legs, and waist securely restrained. *They've really secured me now.* Panic began to rise in his chest as the reality of his situation set in.

At the foot of his bed stood two soldiers, emotionless, hands resting on their weapons. Bert's eyes darted around frantically, searching for a familiar face for Amanda, for anyone who might offer comfort. At first, all he saw were wary glances and tightened grips on rifle stocks. The family he'd been part of now looked at him as a threat, and he felt a deep, aching loneliness that eclipsed even his time on the streets. Then, through the haze of fever and restraints, he became aware of movement around his bed. He forced his eyes to focus on the nearby blurry figures, blinking against the harsh light of the infirmary. Slowly, familiar faces came into view.

Amanda, Samantha, Deacon, Billy, the Professor, and Carl sat in a semicircle around him. Their expressions were a mixture of sorrow, fear, and affection. Bert's heart swelled with emotion as he looked at each of them in turn.

My family is here. Not the little ones, but then I would not want them to see this; it would scare them and scar them.

Amanda stepped forward first, her eyes glistening with unshed tears. "Bert, you've been so brave," she said, her voice barely above a whisper. "Thank you for everything you've done for us."

Samantha nodded, placing a hand on Amanda's shoulder. "We wouldn't have made it this far without you," she added, her usual tough exterior cracking to reveal the pain beneath.

They've each prepared their goodbyes. It must ache for them. I wish I were not the cause of this pain.

Deacon, looking disheveled and with red eyes, spoke next. "You always believed in me, even when others didn't. I won't forget that."

Billy cleared his throat, struggling to maintain his composure. "You've been a rock for this community, Bert. A true friend."

The Professor stepped forward, his scientific detachment faltering. "Your practical wisdom has been invaluable. You will be sorely missed."

Carl, usually so stoic, had tears in his eyes. "You overthrew Nathanial and gave this community its freedom. It's been an honor serving alongside you, Bert. Rest easy now."

He could not speak through the gag, and he was thoroughly restrained, so he just gave them a thumbs-up. He looked at each of them, and a profound realization washed over him. *I did not grow to love these people; I always loved them. I just grew to realize the love that was already there. I had to know them, know our shared existence. The greatest commandment is to love God, for God is in us all. If we would obey just that one greatest of commandments, we would never commit any sins.*

Bert's eyes moved from face to face. Amanda's kind eyes, Samantha's determined set of her jaw, Deacon's youthful yet weathered features, Billy's strong presence, the Professor's thoughtful gaze, and Carl's unwavering loyalty. This was his family, and even in these final moments, he felt a sense of peace knowing he had been part of something so meaningful.

Whatever comes next, I know I can face it, for I have been loved.

A new sensation washed over him, cutting through the fever and emotion. Hunger. Raw, primal, all-consuming hunger. His eyes snapped open, fixing on Billy's exposed forearm.

Bert's mind recoiled in horror, but his body responded with an intense, uncontrollable desire. He wanted to sink his teeth into Billy's flesh, to tear and rend and devour. The urge was overwhelming, drowning out all other thoughts and feelings.

His vision was changing; a milky filter changed his world. It accentuated the red in the flesh around him, the red that indicated the pulsing warmth of life.

Oh! That's why their eyes turn white; it helps them see who is living.

At that moment, the terrible truth crashed over him. He was turning. The virus had won.

Rage exploded through his body, a feral, inhuman fury that obliterated the last vestiges of his humanity. He thrashed against his restraints with newfound strength, the bed frame creaking under the assault. His jaw worked furiously against the gag, desperate to free itself, to bite, to feed.

He focused on his family, who stumbled back in shock and fear. The soldiers raised their weapons. Bert barely registered them now, seeing only prey, only red meat.

In his last flicker of human consciousness, he saw a face, an identity, someone standing behind his family, someone who must not be attacked, someone who was not food, someone who must be obeyed.

The world narrowed to a pinpoint of savage hunger and rage. His body convulsed and strained against the restraints.

A beast that always existed within him was now loose. His lips drew back in a snarl and let out a growl of fury, a growl that called for all his kind to come and feed, a growl that made it clear to everyone present that Bert was gone.

Chapter

MOURNING

Professor Mark Preston - Paradise

The Professor Teaches Science

The makeshift community dining hall of Paradise, usually alive with chatter and the clinking of utensils, lay shrouded in a heavy silence. Bert had once led the community, and many had gathered to mourn him. The chair at the head of the table—Bert's chair—stood empty in his honor.

The Professor's gaze swept across the untouched plates before them. There was not much venison in the venison stew. No one had the heart to eat.

Shafts of late afternoon sunlight cut through the dusty air, illuminating motes that danced, oblivious to the somber mood. The Professor noticed Deacon's hand resting on the table, occasionally twitching toward the empty chair as if to reach for Bert.

The usual sounds of the community going about its daily business seemed muffled and distant as if the entire settlement was holding its breath in shared mourning.

Deacon finally broke the silence, his young voice cracking with emotion: "I can't believe he's gone," he said, staring at his hands. "He was the first adult to really listen to me." The Professor noticed how Deacon's shoulders hunched as if trying to make himself smaller in the face of this loss.

Amanda's hands trembled as she placed them flat on the table, steadying herself. "He saved me on the first day of the outbreak," she said softly. "I would not be here without him. I almost…I almost was frightened of him, the way he looked, rough from the streets."

Samantha, usually so composed, was visibly fighting back tears. "He kept wanting to call me his family," she said, her voice thick with emotion. "And I kept rejecting him because he was a man, and my trauma...oh…I needed to learn you never judge by the group. Never."

The Professor saw guilt etched across Samantha's features.

Billy, who had been staring at Bert's empty chair, spoke next. His voice was hollow, devoid of its usual strength. "His first growl...it broke something in me. Like hope was dying." The Professor had never seen Billy look so defeated, so lost.

Deacon nodded. "That growl..." He paused as if unsure whether to continue. "It had the tone of the voice in it. It didn't say anything, but it sounded like the voice. Sometimes, I feel like we're fighting the supernatural."

The Professor's head snapped up. For him, resorting to explanations that involved magic or the supernatural was dangerous, lazy as well as erroneous thinking. "Every phenomenon we've encountered in the growlers can be explained with science," he said flatly. "Magic and the supernatural are just ways of saying we don't understand something yet."

Deacon looked defiantly at the professor. "Okay, how do they keep moving after they are dead, even if we shoot them in the heart? How do they have a mind controlling them? How is it I can hear them and others cannot? How can this mind reach out from Alameda to instruct that horde?"

Everyone at the table and a number of other community members turned to the professor expectantly.

The professor took a deep breath; he had been doing a lot of thinking about all those questions, and he was ready to respond. "The purpose of the heart is to pump blood for respiration, not all animals have hearts, there are other mechanisms. With growlers, it is the Black; the bacteria fills the mucus membranes of the lungs, the nose, and the mouth; you've seen it dripping out of their mouths, right? The bacteria has flagella, little tails that allow it to transfer energy throughout the dead body. "

There was a murmur among the growing crowd.

The professor continued, "The meta mind, or voice, you hear, is group thought, like…like a flock of starlings or a shoal of fish that seems to make group decisions."

Deacon looked thoughtful but unconvinced.

The professor reached out and put his hands on Deacon's shoulders. "The reason you can hear it, but others cannot, is, I suspect, that when you were cocooned, it added hair cells in your ear to tune your hearing to a specific predefined frequency, something normally humans would not have. This is why the voice has emerged only after the hordes have gone through the cocooning process. The initial phase of the growlers they had no meta mind."

"Why do they want to kill the living?" shouted a man from the crowd.

The professor nodded. "I am speculating a little here, but I believe the virus programmed that behavior."

"Programmed?" shouted the man. "Humans are not computers, Mr. science man."

The professor saw an unlit candle in front of him. He picked it up and threw it at the man, who instinctively caught it. "That catch was a reflex; behavior wired into you before birth, and there are so many others. Have you ever had sex?"

The man in the crowd looked taken aback, but he nodded.

The professor smiled. "Sex is a very complicated behavior, but we are all programmed to seek it out; it's in our programming." He noticed Deacon blushing. "We are computers," he continued. "DNA is our code, and we only think we're in charge."

The professor made a dismissing gesture, signaling he was finished with his explanations.

“Professor,” whispered Deacon. “You didn’t explain how the telepathy works. How does a horde out here know about a horde in Alameda?”

The professor bit his lip. “I haven’t worked that out yet, but I assure you there is a scientific explanation. There always is.”

“Yes sir,” said Deacon, and he looked convinced.

Peter stepped forward from the crowd. He appeared to represent a contingent, and he looked angry. "It ain't natural that these children can communicate with the horde. How do we know they're not spies? How do we know this communication isn’t two-way and that they are knowingly or unknowingly revealing our position and weakness to the enemy?”

“It doesn’t work like that,” said the professor.

Peter shook his head. “That’s what you’d want us to think because he’s part of your little clique, but how do we know for sure? We have had two major horde attacks since that little growler lover arrived.”

The Professor felt a surge of anger at Peter's accusation. He stood up, his chair scraping loudly against the floor. "Deacon has saved this community multiple times. Without him, we wouldn't be here having this conversation."

Peter sneered. "Maybe that's what he wants us to think. Maybe he's leading the hordes right to us."

Murmurs rippled through the crowd. The Professor could see the fear and doubt spreading like a contagion. He looked at Billy for support, but the usually decisive leader seemed lost in his grief.

Amanda stood up next to the Professor. "I've treated Deacon. I've seen his injuries. He's suffered just like the rest of us. How dare you accuse him of being a spy?"

"We're all scared," Samantha added, her voice thick with emotion. "But turning on each other isn't the answer. Bert wouldn't have wanted this."

The mention of Bert's name seemed to quiet the crowd momentarily. The Professor seized the opportunity.

"We're facing unprecedented challenges," he said, his voice steady and clear. "It's natural to seek simple explanations, to look for someone to blame. But the world isn't simple anymore. We need Deacon's abilities. We need to stand together."

He could see some people nodding, but others still looked unconvinced. Peter opened his mouth to argue further, but Billy finally spoke up. "Enough," he said wearily. "We've lost a good man today. This isn't the time for accusations. Everyone, go home. Get some rest. We'll discuss this further when cooler heads prevail."

The crowd began to disperse, but the Professor could hear the continued murmurs of discontent. He watched as Deacon slipped away, shoulders hunched, avoiding eye contact with anyone.

That's a lot for a kid to carry.

As the room emptied, the Professor sank back into his chair, suddenly feeling every one of his years. He looked at the remnants of their core group—Amanda, Samantha, Carl, Billy, and himself—all worn down by loss and fear.

"We need to keep an eye on this situation," he said quietly. "If the community fractures now, we're all doomed."

The others nodded solemnly. As they began to discuss strategies for maintaining unity, the Professor's mind wandered. Despite his confident words earlier, he couldn't shake the nagging doubt about the telepathic connection between distant hordes. There was still so much they didn't understand.

He resolved to double down on his research. They needed answers and fast. As the meeting broke up and he headed back to his lab, a chill ran down his spine. For the briefest moment, he thought he heard a faint, inhuman whisper at the edge of his consciousness. He shook his head, dismissing it as a trick of an overworked mind.

But as he reached his lab and began setting up his equipment, the Professor couldn't quite shake the feeling that they were on the brink of discovering something that would change everything they thought they knew about the growlers—and perhaps about themselves.

How can thoughts be transferred across distances? There's got to be an explanation.

Chapter

THE CULT INSIDER

Amanda – Paradise Hospital Tent

Nurse Amanda Willard awaits arrivals

Amanda entered the hospital tent with the events of the morning weighing heavily on her mind. The morning's attack had left Paradise reeling, and Bert's loss had torn a hole in the community's heart. Now, with tensions rising and trust eroding, she felt as if she were walking on eggshells with every interaction.

She stood at the entrance, her shoulders slumped, her usual smile absent. Her stethoscope was around her neck, ready for another day fighting the war against death, a war all members of her profession knew they eventually lost. Death always marches toward us. It never sleeps, it never pauses, and *it will claim us all one day.*

She paused at the supply boxes, taking a deep breath to center herself. The antiseptic smell that usually brought her comfort now seemed cloying and oppressive. *Focus on the work*, she told herself. *That's what Bert would have done.*

The sound of commotion drew her attention to the hospital entrance. A group of new arrivals were being ushered in, their faces etched with exhaustion and fear. Amanda's trained eye quickly assessed them: a mix of ages, races, and apparent backgrounds, all united by the haggard look of those who had seen too much.

One of the volunteers called out, "Dr. Willard, we've got seven for quarantine and examination."

I keep telling them I am a nurse, not a doctor.

Amanda nodded, pulling on a fresh pair of gloves. "Alright, let's get them settled in exam rooms one through three." That was her joke, as there were no exam rooms, just one big tent that offered no privacy at all. "I'll start with—"

Her words trailed off as her gaze landed on a familiar face among the newcomers. Cassie, the woman Bert's patrol had rescued just before... Amanda swallowed hard, pushing down the sudden surge of resentment that threatened to overwhelm her professional demeanor.

It's not her fault that Bert died. She tried to save him.

Cassie stood apart from the others, her dark skin ashen, her posture sagging with fatigue, eyes darting nervously around the room. She looked even more distressed than during their brief encounter after the attack.

For a moment, Amanda hesitated. A part of her wanted to turn away, to pass Cassie off to another examiner. If they hadn't gone out that day—if they hadn't found her... But Amanda squashed the thought as quickly as it arose. She couldn't blame Cassie for Bert's death. That way lay madness.

Taking another steadying breath, Amanda approached the group. "I'll start with Cassie," she announced, gesturing for the woman to follow her. "The rest of you, please wait outside the tent. I'll get to each of you as quickly as I can."

As Cassie fell into step behind her, Amanda recited the examination protocol in her mind. Check for bites, assess for other health hazards, especially lice, and evaluate overall condition. Standard procedure. She could do this. "Alright, Cassie. Let's get you checked out, shall we? I'll need you to undress."

Cassie took out a small bottle and sprayed a fine mist into the air.

“What was that?” asked Amanda.

Cassie appeared disappointed. “It's been a long time since I showered. I don't want to make you wretch when I peel my clothes off.

Amanda gave her a comforting smile. “Don't worry. I am a nurse, and over this last year, I have gotten used to the odor of survival.”

This woman carries a bottle of perfume through the end of the world so she doesn't smell bad. She restrained herself from shaking her head in wonder.

Cassie began to undress without further hesitation, her movements mechanical and detached. Amanda's professional demeanor faltered for a moment at the sight before her. Cassie's body was a canvas of abuse. Fresh bruises mottled her ribs and arms, and angry red welts crisscrossed her back. She closely examined her whole body; there were no bites, no signs of any kind of infection, nothing that could be considered a danger to the community. Amanda's throat tightened, her medical training warring with her emotional response.

"Oh, Cassie," she breathed, unable to completely mask her shock. "What happened to you?"

Cassie's eyes met Amanda's, a flicker of vulnerability quickly replaced by a guarded expression. "It's nothing," she said flatly. "Just the usual risks of life on the road."

Amanda knew better, but she didn't push. *The growlers aren't the only monsters out there.*

Instead, she continued her examination, her touch gentle as she assessed each injury. "Where have you come from?" she asked softly, hoping to put Cassie at ease.

There was a long pause before Cassie spoke, her voice barely above a whisper. "I escaped from the Phoenix."

Amanda's hands stilled for a moment, her mind racing. *The cult.* The source of so much of their suffering. "You were with them?" she asked, striving to keep her tone neutral.

Cassie nodded, wincing as Amanda probed a particularly tender area. "The Sunol Wilderness Community," she elaborated. "I...I've seen things you wouldn't believe."

As Amanda continued her examination, she gently encouraged Cassie to share more. The woman's words poured out in a quiet, steady stream, painting a picture that made Amanda's blood run cold.

"The cult community there is massive," Cassie explained as Amanda checked her hair for lice and nits. "Thousands of people. But it's the military strength that's truly terrifying. They have at least 7,500 soldiers, all well-trained and heavily armed. Oh, and they have tanks, a whole battalion of them."

Amanda's mind reeled at the implications. "How is that possible?" she asked, struggling to keep the fear from her voice.

Cassie's eyes took on a distant look. "They have the President's support. Remnants of the military are still obeying the chain of command."

Amanda finished her examination in silence, her thoughts churning. As she helped Cassie dress, she knew she had to report this information immediately. The threat to Paradise was far greater than they had imagined.

As Amanda prepared the vaccine, Cassie shrank back. "It's just a vaccine against the black," said Amanda.

Cassie looked terrified. "Where does it come from?"

Amanda put the injection down. "There's nothing to worry about. We've injected thousands by now, and no bad side effects and no one has caught the black after getting it. It really works."

Cassie shook her head. "I don't trust the Phoenix, and you must be getting it from them."

"No." Amanda shook her head. "We researched, designed, and manufactured it ourselves."

There was a long pause as Cassie stared in disbelief. "That would take years. It would take human trials. It would take experienced experts."

Amanda smiled. "We have Professor Mark Preston, who was head of the CDC when the outbreak began."

Cassie nodded. "I remember hearing about him." Her face looked suddenly scared as if she just remembered something. "He was with the President at the beginning. He must be with the Phoenix."

"No, no, the President tried to have him killed." *It must be hard for her to trust anyone.* "You don't have to have the vaccine."

Cassie relaxed and nodded. "Thank you. No vaccine." She closed her eyes and shook her head.

Amanda had to consider the implications of someone refusing the vaccine. No one had refused so far, and so there had been no issue. The Black was such an ever-present fear that people fought to be vaccinated. There would be no herd immunity because the Black floated in the air, but most people in the community were now vaccinated, so it would mostly be her risk. *It's her choice.*

The cult has made her a fearful creature. I wonder what she can tell us about their inner workings. She decided to press further. "Cassie, can you tell me about the cult's leadership? Their ideology?"

Cassie tensed visibly, her eyes darting to the door as if checking for eavesdroppers. After a moment of hesitation, she began to speak, her voice low and strained.

"There's...there's a man. They call him the Genius. Ha! He actually refers to himself as the Genius. He's the one behind the outbreak." Cassie's voice quivered. "His brilliance is matched only by his cruelty. He sees the growlers as his masterpiece, a way to cleanse the world and rebuild it in his image."

Amanda listened intently, not just to Cassie's words but to the tremor in her voice, how her hands shook slightly, and the rapid blinking of her eyes. Her medical training told her that Cassie was exhibiting signs of severe trauma and possibly holding back even more horrific details.

"This Genius," Amanda probed gently, "what else can you tell me about him?"

Cassie opened her mouth as if to speak, then closed it abruptly, shaking her head. "I...I can't. It's too much."

Amanda nodded, recognizing the signs of a traumatized mind protecting itself. She finished restocking the vaccine and helped Cassie dress.

"Cassie," she said softly, "I want you to know that you're safe here in Paradise. We'll protect you." She squeezed her hand reassuringly. "I'm going to arrange for you to speak with our community leaders. They would love to learn as much as you are willing and able to tell us about the cult. But only when you're ready, okay?"

Cassie nodded, a flicker of relief crossing her face. "Thank you, Amanda. I...I'll try to help however I can."

As Cassie left the examination room, Amanda mused on what she had learned. "Next!" she shouted. A man in his early twenties walked in. He looked very unsure of himself. Amanda gave him a reassuring smile. "Undress, please."

Chapter

MARY AND DEACON

Deacon – Deacon's room

Deacon sat alone in his room, examining the equalizer settings on his handheld gaming console. He had several recordings of the meta mind voice, some of which people could hear, but others only he and Leah could hear. He was playing with the idea of lowering the pitch to see if others could hear it.

The community bustled with activity outside, but here, in his room, with his mind focused on the problem, the constant noise faded to a distant hum.

His brow furrowed as he stared out at the barrier of shipping containers and barbed wire that separated them from the dangers beyond. The weight of recent events pressed down on him like a physical force. He could still hear the growls of the last horde attack, still smell the acrid stench of decay. His fingers unconsciously traced the new scar on his forearm, a constant reminder of how close they'd come to being overrun.

I have been lucky to make it this far. Someday, I will end up like Bert. Someday everyone is going to end up like Bert.

Deacon's heart still ached from Bert's death. *It is better not to get close to people; that way, when they die, it won't hurt so much.* He clenched his fist. *He died because my recording of the voice didn't work.* He put both his hands over his face. *It was my fault.* The shame was unbearable. *Why didn't it work? Why did people trust me? How did I fail?*

The responsibility of his role in the community gnawed at him. People looked to him now, expected him to have answers, to hear the voice that could save them all. *I'm just a kid, aren't I? Or is childhood a luxury that we just cannot afford?*

There are so many problems to solve. The cult was still out there, growing stronger. The hordes were evolving, becoming smarter. Here stood the community of Paradise with their ammunition dwindling and their food stores running low, and now the voice didn't work. How long could they hold out? *How long before the fragile peace we've built here crumbles like everything else in this broken world?*

He sighed heavily, running a hand through his unkempt hair.

A soft knock at the container entrance jolted him from his thoughts. Before he could respond, the big metal door creaked open, and Mary slipped inside, closing it quickly behind her. Her sudden appearance startled him, and he fumbled with the gaming console, nearly dropping it.

"Hey, brainiac," Mary said, leaning against the door with an air of forced casualness. Her lips curved into a smile, but Deacon noticed a slight tremor in her hands as she tucked a strand of hair behind her ear. "Figured I'd find you holed up in here, probably inventing a growler-repelling forcefield or something."

He blinked, caught off guard by her unexpected visit. "Uh, hey, Mary. I was just—"

"Being way too serious, as usual," she interrupted her tone teasing but with an undercurrent of nervousness. She pushed off from the door and sauntered toward him, her movements a touch too deliberate to be entirely natural. "You know, if you keep frowning like that, your face might stick that way. Then how will you charm all the ladies in our post-apocalyptic paradise?"

She punctuated her joke with a laugh that sounded slightly forced, her eyes darting around the room before settling back on him. There was an intensity in her gaze that made him shift uncomfortably in his seat.

"Very funny," he muttered, setting aside the console and eyeing her curiously. Something about her behavior seemed off, a tension in her shoulders that belied her attempts at lightheartedness. "Did you need something, or did you just come here to critique my facial expressions?"

Mary's smile faltered for a moment before she hitched it back into place. "Can't a girl just want to hang out with her favorite apocalypse buddy? Maybe I'm here to rescue you from the clutches of boredom and excessive thinking."

He stared at his feet for a moment, thinking how hard it would be to just be friends with her when every atom of his being wanted to be more than friends.

She sat next to him, perched on the edge of his bed. Her casual demeanor seemed like a thin veneer, barely concealing something deeper and more complex beneath the surface.

“If your dad catches us…” he began.

She put her hand on his thigh. “He’s on night patrol. Won’t be back for two hours at least.”

A heavy silence hung in the air for a moment, broken only by the sound of Deacon's quickening breath. Mary's hand on his thigh felt like it was burning through his jeans. Just as he opened his mouth to speak, she reached into her pocket with her free hand.

"I brought something," she said, her voice barely above a whisper.

His eyes widened in shock as she produced a small, square packet. It took him a second to register what it was: a condom. His mouth went dry, and he felt his face flush hot with a mixture of embarrassment and excitement.

She wants to have sex.

This was something he desired beyond anything else. It had been his number-one goal in life for the last two years. Losing his virginity was something he thought about and practiced for every day.

His response was stammered. "Is that... Are you..." He swallowed hard, trying to regain his composure. "Where did you even get that? What did you have to trade?"

A nervous laugh escaped her lips, her cheeks tinged pink. "I heard that the community raided a pharmacy for Amanda. So I asked her if they happened to pick up some protection. It was embarrassing," she admitted, twirling the packet between her fingers. "God, you should've seen her face when I asked for it."

He shook his head in wonder. "But she gave it to you."

"Of course she did. She's a medical professional. Teenagers like us can't be expected to control ourselves. She wants us to avoid unwanted consequences."

Okay…this is happening. She's definitely consenting. She's not been drinking…has she? Who would give her precious alcohol?

Deacon's mind raced, struggling to process this new development. Part of him wanted to laugh at the absurdity of it all—here they were, surrounded by the constant threat of death, and yet they were fumbling through the same awkward teenage moments as if the world hadn't ended.

He remembered his mother and father lecturing him on sex. She told him, "Think about consent, think about disease, think about pregnancy, and think about the law. In blue states, you have to be eighteen; in red states, it's sixteen."

Well, the law doesn't exist now. She's definitely consenting; with the condom, I don't have to think about disease or pregnancy… Although, condoms aren't 100% guaranteed.

"I...wow," he finally managed, his voice cracking slightly. "That's, uh...that's certainly something."

Mary's eyes searched his face, a mix of hope and fear evident in her expression. "Is it...is this okay?" she asked, suddenly sounding much younger and more vulnerable than she had a moment ago. "Do you find me…you know…attractive? Fuck! This shouldn't be so hard. You're a boy, aren't you? You should be all over me."

Deacon smiled at her, but it was a scared smile. "I am incredibly attracted to you. You're everything I ever wanted. I've been desperate to lose my virginity, even before the world fell apart. I think of you so much."

She slowly cracked a lascivious smile. "Do you think about me when you're in the shower?"

His mouth opened in shock at the suggestion.

"Do you think about what you want to do with me?" she added, running a finger down his chest.

He took a deep breath, acutely aware of her proximity, the weight of the moment, and the enormity of what was happening. His heart pounded as he tried to formulate a response, knowing that whatever he said next could change everything between them.

"No girl has ever wanted me," he said. *Why did I say that!* "Why do you want me? Why when all this shit is going down?"

Mary's provocative smile faded, replaced by a look of vulnerability that made her seem even younger than her years. She took a deep breath, her gaze dropping to her hands as they fidgeted with the condom wrapper.

"Why?" she echoed his question softly. "Because everything is so fucked up, Deacon. Everything."

She lifted her eyes to meet his, and he was struck by the pain he saw there. "I can't sleep most nights," Mary continued, her voice barely above a whisper. "Every time I close my eyes, I see them. The growlers. The people we've lost. My mother. My friends. I hear the screams and smell the blood and decay. It's like...it's like I'm drowning in all this darkness, and I can't find my way to the surface."

He reached out instinctively, taking her hand in his. She gripped it tightly, as if it were a lifeline.

"I know I try to act tough," she said, a bitter laugh escaping her lips. "I pretend nothing bothers me. But God, Deacon, I'm so scared all the time. Scared of the growlers, scared of the cult, scared of losing more people I care about. Some days, it's hard to even get out of bed. What's the point, you know? What are we even fighting for?"

Tears welled up in her eyes, and she blinked rapidly, trying to hold them back. "And then I think...maybe this is all there is now. Maybe this is what the rest of our lives will be like. Just surviving, day after day, waiting for the next horrible thing to happen. I keep thinking that everything good is gone. And I can't...I can't bear that thought."

She looked at Deacon, her eyes pleading for understanding. "That's why I'm here. That's why I want this. Because, for once, I want to feel something good. Something that isn't pain or fear or grief. I want to remember that there's still beauty in this world, still pleasure. That life can be more than just surviving."

Mary's grip on Deacon's hand tightened. "I want to feel alive, Deacon. Really alive. Even if it's just for a little while. Is that...is that so wrong?"

The rawness of Mary's confession hung in the air between them. Deacon felt a lump form in his throat, overwhelmed by the depth of her pain and the weight of what she craved. He realized that, in this moment, Mary wasn't just offering her body—she was laying bare her soul, trusting him with her most vulnerable self.

And if I were to give in to my desire, would I be taking advantage of her pain? She's tortured. Or would I be helping her? Oh, who am I kidding? This is something I want, and my mind will come up with any justification to make it okay.

Deacon sat in silence for a moment, processing Mary's words. He felt a deep ache in his chest, a mixture of empathy for her pain and a shared understanding of the fears she'd expressed. Taking a deep breath, he squeezed her hand gently before speaking.

"Mary, I..." he started, his voice thick with emotion. "I get it. I really do. There are nights when I lie awake, replaying every horrible thing we've seen, every person we've lost. I was stuck for days in a pitch-black basement with a dead friend, his dead mother and father, and a massive, angry growler. Sometimes, I wonder if I'm even the same person I was before all this."

He paused, gathering his thoughts. "And the responsibility... God, Mary, sometimes it feels like it's crushing me. Everyone's looking to me for answers, expecting me to save them with this...this voice. What if I fail them? What if I fail you?"

His eyes met hers, and he saw his own vulnerability reflected at him. "I want to feel alive too," he admitted softly. "To feel something other than fear and doubt. And you...you're amazing, Mary. Beautiful, strong, brave. And you're right about what I do in the shower thinking about you. God, I want some pleasure in this world too."

He gestured vaguely between them, a blush creeping up his neck. "But I'm scared too. Not just of the growlers or the cult, but of messing this up. What if we do this, and it changes everything?" He ran a hand through his hair, frustration evident in his voice. "I've never... I mean, I don't know what I'm doing. What if I'm terrible at it? What if you regret it? What if we end up not liking each other, or worse, what if we fall in love and then you … what if something happens to you? I don't know if I could handle that kind of loss."

He looked at her earnestly, his eyes searching hers. "I already care about you so much, Mary. I don't want to take advantage of your pain or do something we might both regret. But I also don't want to push you away when you're reaching out to me. And God knows I want your body so bad I feel like I'm about to explode."

"Jesus, Deacon, it's just sex. You talk too much, and you definitely think too much." She laughed. "Let's just fucking do it."

Deacon's voice softened, filled with a mixture of longing and uncertainty. "I just...I want to do the right thing. For both of us, but I'm not sure what that is."

Mary took a deep breath and sighed. She held the condom up. “I guess this doesn’t negate all possible consequences. But you know what? Sex is irrelevant to whether we end up falling for each other. Just because we have sex doesn’t mean we are in a relationship.”

Deacon’s young mind found that concept hard to grasp. “We could have sex and not be in a relationship?”

Mary looked at him askance. “Well, sure. Just having sex doesn’t mean you are in a relationship. Didn’t you know that?”

He looked at his feet, and his mouth dropped open as he slowly shook his head.

“Anyway, like I said, sex is irrelevant,” said Mary. “We are already in a relationship, really. We know each other, we like each other.”

She leaned back, her eyes fixed on a point somewhere beyond Deacon. "You know, before all this, I used to think I had my whole life planned out. Graduate high school, go to college, find a career, fall in love, get married, have kids. The whole American dream package." She let out a bitter laugh. "Now? Now, I'm not even sure if I'll be alive next week."

He nodded slowly, understanding all too well the weight of uncertainty that hung over their lives. "Yeah, it's like...every day could be our last. It changes everything, doesn't it?"

"Exactly," Mary said, her gaze snapping back to Deacon. "So why are we clinging to old rules that don't make sense anymore? Why deny ourselves comfort, pleasure, connection when it might be the last chance we get?"

He furrowed his brow, considering her words. "I get what you're saying, but...isn't that kind of thinking dangerous? If we just live for the moment without considering consequences, aren't we just adding to the chaos? Aren't we reducing our chances?"

Mary shook her head vehemently. "It's not about being reckless, Deacon. It's about recognizing that life is precious and fleeting. The old world's rules about dating and relationships...they were built for a world with time. We don't have that luxury anymore."

"You know condoms aren't a hundred percent effective, you know," he said.

She sighed. "True. Hell, I was on track to be valedictorian, and you are obviously a genius. Our baby would be a regular Einstein."

"Baby," whispered Deacon, letting that terrifying thought sink in.

She leaned toward him, her lips almost touching his. "Nothing in this world is a hundred percent safe anymore. Survival requires caution, but if we never take any chances … sure, we may survive, but we won't live. What is the point of surviving in order to go from one horrific moment to another without having anything worth actually living for?"

She kissed him with such urgent passion it took him by surprise, and for a moment, he resisted, but then he kissed her back with equal passion.

The fact that he was about to finally have sex just didn't seem real to him. *I don't think I'll last five seconds.*

"Hey there, kids!" came a sharp voice from the container's entrance. Billy walked in, holding a pack of cards.

Mary's eyes widened with shock, and she suddenly moved away from Deacon, sat on his bed, and buttoned up a couple of buttons on her shirt. Deacon grabbed a pillow and sat at the other end of the bed with the pillow on his lap.

"What are you doing here!" shouted Mary.

"Your father told me you both like playing cards and asked me to come and teach you some new games while he's out on patrol."

Mary groaned.

"I can see you like playing new games," Billy said, sitting between them and holding up the cards. "I'll teach you Texas Holdem."

Deacon and Mary both had similar expressions. Their lips were drawn tight in frustration and anger. Billy wore the broadest of smiles.

Chapter

Spy

Amanda and the Professor

Amanda wiped the sweat from her brow as she finished changing a patient's bandages. *I guess the days of air-conditioned treatment rooms are gone,* she thought wearily. The stuffy air inside the medical tent was thick with the smell of alcohol and sweat. She turned to the Professor, who was inventorying their dwindling medical supplies.

"You know, Professor," Amanda said with a wry smile, "I never thought I'd miss the sound of heart monitors and ventilators. It's too quiet in here."

The Professor looked up from his clipboard, a rueful expression on his face. "I imagine this is quite different from your previous workplace, Amanda."

She nodded, gesturing around the sparse tent. "You could say that. Before all this, I worked in a state-of-the-art emergency room.

Now look at us—using bedsheets as dividers and hoping our last bottle of painkillers doesn't run out before the next supply run."

"Yet you've managed to save countless," the Professor remarked, his tone admiring.

"I lost a few too," she said and closed her eyes momentarily. She sighed, running her hand along a makeshift operating table—little more than wooden planks on sawhorses. "We do what we can. What frustrates me is losing a patient when I could have easily saved them if I just had the right equipment or drug. Last week, I lost a man because of an infection from an untreated cavity. He died from toothache because we had no antibiotics."

"We do what we can," the Professor said firmly. "This tent, as humble as it is, has become the lifeline of our community. Your skills and adaptability are worth more than any fancy equipment."

"I keep telling people I'm a nurse, not a doctor," she said.

The Professor smiled. "And they keep calling you doctor. It's a mark of respect."

Amanda shook her head. "Nurses should have as much respect from them as doctors. We work twice as hard, and we know more about the practicalities of treatment."

He put his clipboard down. "What would you say is your number one need, and don't say everything."

"I am no surgeon, but I am doing surgery. Yesterday, a rat ran over my feet while I was performing an appendectomy on an unanesthetized patient. If we get a container dedicated to surgery, and we scavenge some bleach and acetone, I could make chloroform; we need to find antibiotics… and any pain medications… and—”

“Stop.” He picked up his clipboard again. I think we can requisition a container, though it will mean throwing a couple of families back into tent city, which won’t make you popular. For now, everyone has been ordered to prioritize food scavenging.”

She sighed. “Well, when people are looking for food, tell them to keep their eyes out for medicines, bleach, and acetone.”

“I’ll tell the council.” The professor gave her a grim smile.

Her mind wandered to the events of the past few weeks. The loss of Bert still stung, a constant ache that threatened to overwhelm her in quiet moments. Now, with tensions rising in the community and the looming threat of both the cult and the evolving growlers, she felt as though she were standing on the edge of a precipice, one strong gust away from toppling over.

Amanda sat down. “When we left the bunker to come here, we were supposed to defeat the cult, defeat the growlers, and start rebuilding society, but it sounds like the growlers are regrouping, and the cult still has the backing of what’s left of the U.S. army, and our community has no sense of unity, and we’re low on food.”

“Society is always three meals away from collapse,” said the professor. “We are activating all the scavenging parties we can.”

She knew that Deacon was going with Billy on a scavenging expedition. She balled her fist; she didn’t agree with sending

Deacon out. He was just a kid, and he was too valuable. His brain was the community's most precious resource.

A commotion at the entrance snapped her out of her thoughts. Her heart sank as she saw Cassie being half-carried into the hospital, her face swollen and bruised. A gruff-looking man supported her, his expression a mix of disgust and reluctant concern.

"What in the world happened?" Amanda demanded, rushing to help Cassie onto the examination table. Her trained eye quickly cataloged the injuries: contusions on the face and arms, bruised ribs, split lip...

The man supporting Cassie grunted, his calloused hands releasing her gently onto the table. "Found her getting beaten by a mob near the eastern perimeter. They said she was ex-cult." His eyes hardened, a flicker of pain crossing his weathered features. "Lost my brother to those bastards. But I couldn't stand seeing a woman get pummeled like that, cult or no cult."

"That's ridiculous," said Amanda. "We have so many ex-cult members here. We welcome all."

The man snorted. "Yeah, but she was an early member, a true believer. Without her type, there would be no growlers."

Amanda's hands shook with a mixture of anger and professional determination as she began examining Cassie's injuries more closely. "This is unacceptable," she muttered, more to herself than anyone else. "We can't allow vigilante justice in Paradise. We're supposed to be better than this."

As she worked, cleaning wounds and assessing the damage, Amanda's mind raced. *How has it come to this? Paradise is supposed to be a haven. Three meals away from collapse is right. Human nature is like growler nature under the façade.*

"Cassie," Amanda said softly, meeting the battered woman's eyes. "Can you tell me what happened?"

Cassie winced as Amanda probed a particularly tender area on her ribs. "I...I was just walking," she began, her voice barely above a whisper. "Someone recognized me from...before. Started shouting that I was a cultist spy. Before I knew it, there was a crowd. They were so angry..."

Amanda felt a surge of protective fury. "This isn't right. We'll find who did this. There have to be consequences, or we're no better than—"

The professor shook his head. "I understand your feelings, Amanda. Truly, I do. But our community isn't cohesive enough yet to implement universal rights and a robust justice system. We have to tread carefully." He adjusted his glasses, a habit Amanda had come to recognize as a sign of his discomfort. "The cult has everyone on edge. If we push too hard, too fast, we risk fracturing what little stability we've managed to achieve."

Amanda opened her mouth to argue, but Cassie's soft voice interrupted. "It's okay. Really. I...I understand their anger. After everything the cult has done..." She trailed off, wincing as she tried to sit up straighter. "I just don't feel safe here anymore."

The Professor's eyebrows rose, his keen mind clearly processing this new information. "You're considering leaving?"

The man who had rescued her and had been standing silently by the entrance scoffed. "Pfft! She wants to go back to the cult. Maybe the mob was right to beat her if she's running back to those psychos." His words were harsh, but Amanda could hear the undercurrent of pain in his voice. How many others in Paradise had lost loved ones to the cult's influence?

Cassie flinched at the man's words, and Amanda felt a surge of empathy. She reached out, gently squeezing Cassie's hand. "You don't have to go anywhere. We can protect you here."

Cassie shook her head, tears welling in her eyes. "I hate the cult. I hate what they stand for, what they've done. But..." She looked down to the ground. "Where else can I go? At least there, I knew my place. Here, I'm just a reminder of everything people have lost."

A tense silence fell over the room. Amanda felt torn. She knew they could not really protect Cassie, not when so many in the community had so much reason to hate the cult. But to send her back to the cult was too harsh, especially considering she was a woman. Amanda knew the role women played in the cult: subservient breeders. She looked at the Professor, hoping he might have a solution, but he seemed lost in thought, his brow furrowed in concentration.

It was the man by the entrance who broke the silence, his gruff voice almost a whisper. "What if...what she went back as a spy?"

All eyes in the room turned to him, and he shifted uncomfortably under their gaze. "Look, I'm not saying I trust her. But if she really hates the cult as much as she says, maybe she could do some good. Earn her place here by helping us fight them. Then she could rejoin us and become part of the Paradise family."

Amanda's eyes widened at the suggestion. "That's far too dangerous," she protested. "We can't ask someone to put themselves in that kind of risk. My friends and I can protect you here, Cassie. We'll make the others understand."

Even as Amanda spoke, she noticed a change come over Cassie. The woman seemed to sit up straighter, a spark of something—purpose, perhaps—igniting in her eyes.

"I would like a family," Cassie murmured, and Amanda's heart clenched. The words were so similar to what Bert used to say, his constant refrain about family and belonging.

Cassie must feel so alone.

The Professor leaned forward. "There would be a great deal to be gained from inside information," he mused. "The cult's structure, their plans, their weaknesses... But the risks are enormous. If they were to discover your true allegiance..."

Amanda's mouth opened in shock. "You can't be serious. Sending her back to those…those…evil…brutes." Words failed her. *The marks on her body when she arrived…*

She watched Cassie closely, seeing the internal struggle play out across her face: the desire for acceptance warring with fear, the need to atone, battling with self-preservation. It was a battle Amanda knew all too well—the constant weighing of personal safety against the greater good in this dangerous new world.

"Cassie," Amanda said softly, "you don't have to do this." She grabbed both of Cassie's hands. "You really do not have to go."

Cassie met Amanda's gaze, and at that moment, Amanda saw a strength she hadn't noticed before. "But I do," Cassie replied. "I owe it to myself and to all the people the cult has hurt. If I can help stop them, even a little...maybe I can start to make things right." Finally, Cassie nodded, her decision made. "I'll do it. I'll spy for you."

Amanda felt a complex mix of emotions—relief that they might gain a crucial advantage, guilt at putting Cassie in such danger, and grudging admiration for the woman's courage.

The Professor, ever practical, immediately began outlining a plan. "We'll need to establish a secure method of communication. Perhaps a radio with an encrypted frequency, and you'll need a reason for why you were separated from the cult."

Cassie interrupted. "And they'll search me when I return. Thoroughly. I'll have to bury a radio outside their community and retrieve it later when I can sneak out. We should have code words. I will tell them I got chased by growlers, which isn't far from the truth and will be easy to believe. They're egomaniacs; they don't think people can lack faith in them."

Amanda marveled at Cassie's quick thinking. It was clear she had valuable insider knowledge that could prove crucial to their survival.

As they fine-tuned the details of the plan, Amanda's mind raced. Were they doing the right thing? The ethical implications were staggering. They were essentially sending Cassie back into an abusive, dangerous situation. But the potential impact on their fight against the cult and the growlers... It could mean the difference between survival and annihilation for Paradise.

"We'll need to prepare you," the Professor said. "Give you some basic training in espionage techniques and emergency protocols… though in all honesty, there's little we can do to rescue you if they are as strong as you say."

Cassie nodded, a grim determination settling over her features. "I'll need to rough myself up a bit more too. Make it look like I barely escaped the mob. They'll be suspicious if I show up looking too well-cared for."

The casual way Cassie spoke about inflicting further harm on herself made Amanda's stomach churn. "I don't like this," she said, knowing even as she spoke that it wouldn't change anything.

Amanda found herself stepping back as the others continued to plan. She felt overwhelmed by the weight of what they were setting in motion. She moved to the entrance, staring out at the bustling community of Paradise—people going about their daily lives, unaware of the dangerous gambit being planned just a few feet away.

She felt a presence beside her and turned to see the Professor. He looked older than she'd ever seen him, the lines on his face deepened by worry.

"Are we making a huge mistake?" she asked softly, voicing the fear that had been gnawing at her since Cassie agreed to the plan.

The Professor sighed heavily, removing his glasses to rub his tired eyes. "Possibly," he admitted. "But in this new world, Amanda, sometimes we have to make hard choices."

"At what cost, though?" Amanda pressed. "We're gambling with her life, and even if she succeeds, what does it say about us that we're willing to send someone back into a traumatic situation for our own gain? We're losing the moral high ground."

The Professor was quiet for a long moment, his gaze fixed on the scene outside. "It says that we're desperate," he finally replied. "That we're human, with all the flaws and compromises that entails. It also says that we still have hope. Hope that one person's bravery can make a difference. Hope that we can outsmart our enemies and build a better future."

He turned to Amanda, placing a comforting hand on her shoulder. "We can't know if this is the right choice, but it's the choice we've made. All we can do now is support Cassie as best we can and hope that it pays off."

A man entered the hospital. He was a short man, Cassie recognized as someone who had helped her on a few occasions. *What was his name?* She desperately tried to remember. *Chuck!*

"Hi, Doctor," said Chuck. "I was told to look out for bleach and nail polish." He held up two large plastic bottles.

"Oh, Chuck, you angel," she said.

"It's amazing how few looters take bleach and nail polish," he said wryly. "They all seem to be interested in silly things like food."

"Believe me, Chuck. I will have my uses for this."

The Professor led Cassie away.

Amanda looked at the bottles. Making chloroform was a very dangerous process, and she began to map out how to do it.

Chapter

THE DRONE MISSION

The Hangar

The squawk of birds and the slapping of waves against hulls were the only sounds as Deacon, and Billy maneuvered their small craft between the abandoned boats dotting the bay. The morning mist clung to the water's surface, lending an eerie quality to their scavenging mission.

I am so glad to be away from Paradise for a while, Deacon thought. *Too many people are giving me the stink eye these days, and that's not even counting Sven, who, let's face it, has reason.* Mary had made it clear she was ready to end Deacon's virginity, and Deacon was not resistant to the idea. *If we're careful, there needn't be any consequences. Safe sex, they call it.* That thought made Deacon smile because Billy had recently asked him if he knew about safe sex. "Yes, I know about safe sex," Deacon had replied. "It means making sure her father doesn't find out." Billy had not seen the humor.

He felt that in the weeks since Bert's death the cohesion of the community was failing. Everyone knew the crops would be woefully insufficient, and hunting and scavenging were getting harder.

Deacon's eyes scanned the vessels around them, searching for any sign of useful supplies. His stomach growled, reminding him of their primary objective: food. Paradise's stores were running dangerously low. Amanda had put everyone on a 400-calorie-a-day diet after acknowledging that 1200 calories was a starvation diet. *We must find food.*

"Over there," Billy whispered, pointing at a sleek yacht listing slightly to one side.

Deacon appraised it. The yacht was expensive-looking, so if there was food, it'd likely be of good quality.

They approached cautiously, always wary of potential threats—human or growler. As they climbed aboard, Deacon's foot slipped on the dew-slicked deck. Billy caught his arm, steadying him with a grunt.

"Sorry," Deacon whispered.

I have got to be less clumsy. I think I'm going through a growth spurt or something.

The yacht's cabin was a mess of overturned furniture and scattered belongings. Deacon's heart sank as he realized the food stores had long since been raided. But then, tucked beneath an overturned table, he spotted something.

"Billy," he called softly, reaching for the object. "Look."

In his hands was a revolver, its metal cool and heavy. Deacon checked the cylinder—six bullets.

I can't imagine how raiders didn't find that, if they found the food.

Billy nodded approvingly. "Good find, kid. But it's not gonna fill our bellies."

They continued their search, finding little else of value. As they prepared to leave, Deacon's gaze was drawn to a boat further out—its deck adorned with solar panels glinting in the emerging sunlight.

"Billy," Deacon said, excitement creeping into his voice. "Solar panels over there." There didn't need to be any explanation. Solar panels may not fill stomachs, but the power they provided had a myriad of uses.

Billy followed his gaze and nodded. "They look heavy, but as long as you do the carrying, let's go."

Deacon smiled. They boarded the boat, quickly assessing its condition. It had been raided already. There was no food, no weapons or ammunition, but whoever had raided it had left the solar panels. Deacon explored the cabin. His breath caught as he opened a storage locker.

"Billy!" he called out. "You're not going to believe this."

Nestled in protective foam was a sleek, high-end drone. Deacon carefully lifted it out, his mind racing with possibilities.

"We're not here to get you toys, Deacon," said Billy.

Deacon frowned. "A drone can be very useful. It could give us a bird's eye view of a battlefield; it could spot enemies far away." He took it out of the box and examined it closely.

"Does it work?" Billy asked.

"If the solar panels are working, I could try charging it and find out."

Deacon spent the next couple of minutes preparing and plugging the drone in to charge. "The battery was already 70% charged. It won't take long."

"Let's search the neighboring boats while we wait," said Billy.

The next boat they spied was a 20-foot center console with a faded white hull. It rocked gently with the rhythm of the waves and looked untouched.

"Stay close," Billy murmured, hefting his ax in his right hand and his gun in his left. His shoes squeaked as he stepped onto the deck.

Deacon nodded, gripping his ax tightly. He kept his gun holstered as he climbed aboard. There was a faint whiff of something rotten. He looked at Billy with eyebrows raised. "Do you smell that?" he mouthed silently. Billy nodded, signaling for Deacon to stay quiet. They moved forward cautiously.

Deacon peered into the cockpit, the seats cracked and sun-faded but otherwise empty. "Clear," he whispered.

Billy nodded and gestured toward the small storage cabin at the front of the boat. "Check in there," he said, his voice low.

Deacon swallowed and moved to the cabin door, gripping the handle with one hand while holding his ax in the other. He twisted the handle and pushed the door open slowly, the hinges groaning in protest.

A growler lunged at him from the darkness within, its decaying hands swiping wildly. Deacon reacted instinctively, thrusting his ax into the creature's head, but the blow was not deep enough, so the growler kept coming, driven by the insatiable hunger that had overtaken its mind. Billy fired his gun and took the head clean off the creature. It collapsed with a sickening crunch, its body twitching before going still.

Deacon grabbed his ears. *Christ!* There was a high-pitched screaming sound in his ears.

Billy reached up and touched the side of Deacon's face. His hand came away with blood. "Can you hear me?" he shouted.

Deacon nodded. "Yeah. Fuck, your gun was too close to my ear when you fired. Is that blood from my ear?"

Billy nodded. "I know it was too close, but I couldn't risk that thing biting you."

The high-pitched scream in his ears was fading. "You could have deafened me, but you did what you had to do." Deacon panted, staring down at the lifeless growler. "That was close," he muttered, wiping his brow with the back of his hand.

Billy clapped him on the shoulder. "I shouldn't have told you to open that door. I should have done it."

Deacon shook his head. "Then you'd be bitten because I wasn't holding my gun. I thought I could deal with any threat with my ax."

"It was a big brute with a thick skull," said Billy.

Deacon nodded, his adrenaline still surging. They both took a moment to catch their breath before turning their attention back to the cabin. Inside, the space was cramped and smelled strongly of death. A small table was bolted to the floor, with a few cupboards overhead.

They searched quickly but thoroughly. In one of the cupboards, Deacon found two small packets of peanuts. He held them up, grinning. "Hey, look at this."

Billy's eyes lit up, and he snatched one of the packets. "Well, well. Let's see if they're any good." He tore one open and popped a few peanuts into his mouth, chewing slowly. "Still fresh."

Deacon did the same with the other bag, savoring the salty taste. It was the first real food they'd found in days that wasn't canned or dried beyond recognition.

Billy rifled through another cupboard, grinning as he pulled out two bottles of beer. "Jackpot," he said, handing one to Deacon.

Deacon hesitated for only a moment before twisting off the cap and taking a long swig. The beer was warm, but it went down easy, soothing his parched throat. They both leaned against the side of the boat, savoring the small luxury.

"Tut tut tut," said Deacon. "Giving a beer to a minor. You could get arrested for such behavior."

Billy smiled. "Times have changed."

Once the bottles were empty, Deacon had a sudden realization. "We're supposed to bring back anything with calories and share it with the community." The guilt began to settle in. He glanced at Billy, who was staring out over the water with a troubled look on his face.

"We should've taken these back to the community," Deacon repeated quietly, voicing what they were both thinking.

Billy sighed, nodding. "Yeah, we should've." He stared down at the empty bottle in his hand. "Damn, that was good, though. I forgot how good beer could taste."

They were about to leave when Deacon's eyes fell on the growler they had killed. It lay twisted on the deck, its body already beginning to stiffen in the cool morning air. Deacon noticed something odd—a bulge beneath the tattered jacket it wore. He crouched down and pulled the jacket aside, revealing a worn backpack strapped to the growler's back.

"Billy, look at this," Deacon said, unzipping the backpack. Inside, they found an unexpected treasure: cans of food, packets of dried meat, a couple of water bottles, and even a few candy bars.

"Must've been scavenging when it got bit," Billy muttered, eyes widening at the haul. "Damn, this is a good find."

Deacon couldn't help but laugh, a mix of relief and disbelief. "I guess we won't have to feel guilty after all."

Deacon put the contents into his own backpack. "Let's see if the battery has charged."

Billy nodded. The guilt of their indulgence was still there, but it was tempered by the knowledge that they were bringing back something much more valuable.

Deacon checked, and the drone's battery was now fully charged, so he powered it up, grinning as its lights blinked to life. "Awesome. I already know how I want to use it."

Billy raised an eyebrow.

"We sail down to Alameda and fly this puppy through that closed-down naval station where I think the mega horde is." Deacon paused, expecting Billy to shoot down his idea.

Billy mused in silence for several minutes; the way he chewed his lip made him look very conflicted. Finally, he clapped Deacon on the shoulder, a rare smile breaking through his usual stoic expression. "Alright, kid. Looks like we've got ourselves a side quest."

Deacon grinned back. He had to admit to himself the kid in him wanted to play with the drone, but he did think it was a good idea to recon the naval station.

Twenty minutes later, they had started their journey south toward Alameda. The sun had burned off the morning mist, promising a scorching day.

Billy steered the boat with one hand, the other resting on his knee. "You did good back there," he said, breaking the silence. "Handled yourself well with that growler, not that I doubted you."

Deacon shrugged, staring out at the water. "I guess. Just doing what we have to."

Billy nodded, his gaze still fixed on the horizon. "Uh-huh. That's the thing, kid. This world we're living in now doesn't come with a rulebook. You gotta figure it out as you go, and you are quick-witted."

Deacon glanced over at Billy, waiting for him to continue. Billy had a way of talking in circles, but there was usually something worth hearing in what he said.

"Take Mary, for example," Billy went on.

Oh God, not another lecture on sex.

Billy continued. "No one in Paradise is blind to what's been going on between you two, especially Sven."

Deacon felt his face heat up. *It is impossible to keep secrets in Paradise. It's like a small town.*

"Look, I'm not saying don't go after what you want," Billy said, his tone gentle but firm. "But you gotta think ahead. In this world, every action has consequences, and it's not just about you. It's about her too. You gotta be sure, and you gotta be careful."

"It's hard to go after what I want when you sit in between us with a pack of cards."

Billy chuckled. "Yeah, that must have been a little frustrating."

"And I should point out…" Deacon hesitated. "Yeah, I should point out that you are … well… you are doing it with two women right now."

"But me, Samantha, and Amanda are fully grown adults."

Deacon swallowed, nodding slowly. "I know, Billy. It's just… it's hard. Everything's different now. It's like nothing matters anymore, but at the same time, everything matters more."

Billy gave a low chuckle. "That's a good way to put it. But listen, just because things are different doesn't mean we throw away what's right. We still gotta live with ourselves at the end of the day. And we still gotta live with the people around us."

They lapsed into silence, the only sound the steady swoosh of the boat cutting its way through the water and the occasional call of a seagull overhead. Deacon let Billy's words sink in. He knew the older man was right, but that didn't make things any easier. He had no intention of resisting his desires the next time he and Mary had an opportunity.

Deacon noticed Billy looking up and followed his gaze. They were about to pass under the bay bridge. Part of the bridge had been blown up, and there was a large gap in the span. An abandoned tank sat facing Oakland. A crowd of growlers had gathered on the San Francisco side of the span.

"Wow," said Billy. "There's a lot of them on the bridge. All on one side of the span for some reason."

Deacon stared at the horde. "They're trying to get to the naval base, but they don't have the individual intelligence to realize they have to go the long way. They're confused."

"You really can read their minds." Billy stared at him.

His stare made Deacon uncomfortable. "No, I am just interpreting their actions. They've seen us. They know we're alive. Shit!"

The growlers were jumping off the bridge at them. The bodies started falling around the boat.

"Fuck!" shouted Billy. "I'm sparking up the engine. We got to get through here quick."

There was only about a gallon in the tank; it was only for emergencies, but Deacon realized this probably qualified. Billy turned the key, but nothing happened.

Deacon looked at Billy. "Has the fuel gone bad? We should have tested it before…"

A massive body slammed into the deck, splattering limbs and bones in all directions.

"Jesus!" said Deacon. The bodies were exploding in the water all around them. The bridge was almost 200 feet above them.

"What are they thinking?" shouted Billy.

Deacon shook his head. "They don't think… well… not really. They just have instinct, and right now, their instinct is to attack us."

"But what about the meta-mind? I thought it was smart." Billy sounded scared and confused.

"It doesn't work like that," shouted Deacon as another body ricocheted off the hull, taking some of the railing with it into the bay. "Each growler is dumb as a rock. Only the horde itself can act with … look, the horde is turning away; it's moving toward San Francisco. Like I said, as a group, they can do smart things, but individually, they just act on instinct."

The bodies stopped falling.

"It's a bit like regular people, only in reverse," mused Billy.

"What?" Deacon was confused.

"Individually, people can be very smart, but large groups tend to become really dumb."

I am sure what he said is profound, but I don't really get it, thought Deacon.

"There!" Billy pointed to the left. "Just past that outcrop, we turn into the naval base."

As they approached the narrow channel leading into the Alameda marina, the water became choppier. Deacon's thoughts drifted back to Mary, to the way she smiled at him when they were alone, and to the guilt that gnawed at him whenever he thought about Sven. *I can't believe how much I think about that girl. We just escaped growlers falling out of the sky and I am immediately thinking about getting laid. Is something wrong with me?*

Billy glanced at him out of the corner of his eye. "Just keep your eye out for the next nasty surprise."

Deacon nodded, appreciating the advice even though he wasn't sure what to do with it yet.

Okay we are here, where the horde should be. This is it. Everything rides on what we find here.

He could feel Billy's eyes on him, watching, assessing. The weight of expectation pressed down on Deacon's shoulders like a physical burden. He'd been so sure, so convinced when he'd told the others about the voice, about the horde gathering at the naval base.

The memory of that meeting flashed through his mind. The skeptical looks, the whispers, the barely concealed eye-rolls from some. Only a few had believed him outright. Others had humored him, probably out of respect for his past contributions. And then there were those who thought he'd finally cracked under the pressure.

"Poor Deacon," he imagined them saying. "The stress finally got to him. Hearing voices now, is he?"

A bitter taste rose in his throat. What if they were right? What if this was a wild goose chase, nothing more than the product of a mind stretched to its breaking point?

Deacon's eyes flicked to the coastline, searching for any sign of movement, any hint of the massive horde he'd promised would be there. The shoreline remained stubbornly, maddeningly empty.

Christ, what if there's nothing here? What then?

The implications made his stomach churn. If he was wrong, it wasn't just his pride on the line. It was his credibility, his position in the community. The trust people had placed in him. All of it could evaporate in an instant.

Surely I should be relieved there's no horde. That means we're safe. God, what would Mary think? He'd confided in her, shared his fears and his conviction about what was coming. The memory of her touch, her reassuring words, now felt like a knife twisting in his gut. If this turned out to be nothing more than a delusion, how could she ever look at him the same way again?

Maybe I am crazy. Maybe the stress, the constant fear, the weight of responsibility... maybe it's all finally broken something in my mind. Do crazy people know they are crazy?

The thought sent a chill down his spine. He'd seen it happen to others, watched as the harsh reality of their new world chipped away at sanity until there was nothing left but a shell. He'd always prided himself on staying grounded, on being a rock for others to lean on. But now...

He shook his head, trying to dispel the doubts that threatened to overwhelm him. He couldn't afford to second-guess himself, not now. Too much was riding on this.

If I'm right, we might have a chance to prepare, to survive what's coming. If I'm wrong...well then I am losing my mind.

Deacon's resolve hardened. One way or another, he was about to get answers. He just prayed he was strong enough to face them, whatever they might be.

"We're almost there," he said, breaking the tense silence that had fallen between him and Billy. His voice sounded strange to his own ears, tight with a mix of anticipation and dread.

Billy nodded, his expression unreadable. "Whatever we find, Deacon, we'll deal with it. Together."

Deacon managed a tight smile, grateful for the support even as doubt gnawed at him. As they prepared to drop anchor, he took a deep breath, steeling himself for what lay ahead.

This is it. No turning back now.

The boat's engine sputtered to silence as they anchored thirty feet from the naval base's perimeter. The sudden quiet was oppressive, broken only by the gentle lapping of waves against the hull. Deacon's eyes scanned the shoreline, searching desperately for any sign of movement.

Nothing. No shambling figures. No guttural moans carried on the salt-tinged breeze.

Billy's gaze bore into Deacon, a mix of concern and something else—doubt, maybe even pity. Deacon's stomach clenched. *That's how people look at crazy people. He thinks I'm losing it. That the voice was just a delusion.*

Deacon's hands trembled as he gripped the boat's railing. He closed his eyes, listening intently. No growls. No snarls. No sound of decaying limbs dragging across concrete. Just the wind and the waves, indifferent to his inner turmoil.

He sniffed the air. The bay smelled of mud and fish. It was not the familiar odor of rotting flesh that came from growlers.

Deacon's jaw clenched. *No. I'm not crazy. There's something here. There has to be.*

He shook his head, as if trying to dislodge the creeping tendrils of self-doubt. His voice was steadier than he felt when he spoke. "Let's take a closer look."

With practiced movements that belied his inner uncertainty, Deacon prepared the drone. The blades whirred to life. As it rose into the air, Deacon knew they were about to uncover something that would change everything.

For better or worse, we're about to find out the truth.

As the drone rose above the boat's deck, Deacon's heart raced. He guided it toward the naval base, his eyes glued to the tablet displaying the live feed. Billy leaned in close, his breath tense with anticipation.

The drone soared over the perimeter of the base, revealing...nothing. Empty streets, abandoned vehicles, and an eerie silence greeted them. There were no hordes, no signs of the massive gathering.

"I don't understand," Deacon muttered, a cold doubt creeping into his gut. "There should be thousands of them here, tens of thousands or hundreds of thousands."

Billy's expression tightened. "Maybe they've moved on already?"

Or maybe I need psychiatric help. People who hear voices need antipsychotic medications. That's all I need, having lost everything and everyone, to lose my mind.

He shook his head, frustration and uncertainty warring within him. Had he imagined it all? Was the voice just a product of his overwrought mind, his desperate desire to be useful to the community? *How am I going to explain this to everyone?*

"Let's check inside the structures," Billy suggested, his tone gentle. "They might be sheltering from the sun."

Nodding, Deacon guided the drone toward one of the massive hangars. The huge doors were partially open, offering more than enough space for the drone to fly inside. The feed adjusted to the dimmer light. Deacon's breath caught in his throat.

What the hell?

At first, his brain couldn't process what he was seeing. The hangar floor writhed, a mass of undulating white fibers stretching as far as the drone's camera could capture. It was like staring into a pit of maggots, if maggots grew to monstrous proportions.

He swallowed hard, an acrid taste burning his esophagus.

"Oh my God," Billy whispered.

Deacon's fingers trembled as he guided the drone lower. The sea of white resolved into individual cocoons, each one easily large enough to encase a human body. No, not a human body. A growler.

The entire floor, stretching as far as the drone's camera could see, was blanketed with growlers in cocoons. Thousands upon thousands of them, packed tightly together, their forms barely visible beneath the white, fibrous material.

Deacon's hands shook as he maneuvered the drone for a better view. His mind recoiled from the implications, but he couldn't look away. The cocoons pulsed in unison, a rhythm that bored into his skull like a drill. With each throb, Deacon could swear he felt something pushing against the edges of his consciousness, probing, searching. It was both mesmerizing and terrifying.

Billy's face had gone pale. "We need to get this footage back to Paradise immediately. The Professor needs to see this. We need to get out of here." His voice was tight. "We've seen enough."

Have we? Or are we just scratching the surface of this nightmare?

Deacon prepared to guide the drone out of the hangar, but a sudden movement caught his eye. Near the center of the mass of cocoons, one began to split open. A growler, its skin pale and almost translucent, began to emerge.

"Billy, look!" Deacon exclaimed. "The professor says the cocoons heal them. This one looks in perfect shape, like it's never been injured."

They watched in horrified fascination as the creature pulled itself free of the cocoon. Its movements were fluid and graceful, like an athlete in their prime. It turned its face toward the drone. Deacon felt a chill run down his spine. Its eyes seemed to focus directly on the camera, a hint of intelligence gleaming in their depths.

This isn't right. Growlers are supposed to be clumsy, decaying. This one looks... whole.

A high-pitched whine filled the air, stabbing into Deacon's ears like needles. He winced, his vision blurring. And then...

Voices.

They crashed over him like a tsunami, a cacophony of whispers that threatened to drown out his own thoughts. He gripped the edge of the boat, his knuckles turning white as he fought to stay upright.

Make it stop. Please, make it stop.

But it didn't stop. The whispers coalesced, forming words, intentions, plans. Deacon's mind reeled as understanding flooded in.

"Billy," Deacon said, his voice trembling, "I can hear it, the voice...it's not just one. It's all of them, like a choir harmonizing."

Billy's eyes widened, a mix of fascination and skepticism crossing his face. "What are they saying?"

They're waiting," he gasped, the words tearing from his throat. "Gathering strength. They want... they need..."

Billy gripped his shoulder, steadying him. "What, Deacon? What do they need?"

Deacon looked up, meeting Billy's gaze. He saw his own terror reflected back at him, magnified tenfold.

"Numbers," Deacon whispered. "A million, at least. And then..." He trailed off, the full weight of the revelation crushing down on him.

How do I tell him? How do I put this horror into words?

"Then what?" Billy pressed, his fingers digging into Deacon's flesh.

Deacon swallowed, tasting copper. Had he bitten his tongue? He couldn't remember.

"They're coming for us. All of us. Paradise..." His voice cracked. "We're ground zero."

The silence that followed was absolute. Even the waves seemed to hold their breath.

Am I going insane? Or is the world so far beyond sanity that this is our new reality?

Doubt gnawed at the edges of Deacon's mind. But as he looked back at the tablet, at the sea of cocoons and the newly emerged growler still staring directly at them, he knew. This was real. This was happening.

And they were woefully, catastrophically unprepared.

"We need to warn everyone," Deacon said, his voice hollow. "But how do we prepare for this? How do we fight an enemy that's evolving, strategizing, amassing in numbers we can't even comprehend?"

Billy didn't answer. There was no answer to give.

As they retrieved the drone and set course back to Paradise, Deacon's mind raced. The weight of their discovery pressed down on him, threatening to crush his very soul.

We thought we were rebuilding. We thought we had a chance.

He stared out at the choppy waters, each wave a grim reminder of the tidal wave of horror that was coming.

We were wrong. So very, very wrong.

Paradise. It wasn't just at risk. It was a target. It wasn't a home anymore, it was a trap. All their building, planting, planning and dreaming had all been pointless. All the arguments, all the battles, all the sacrifice, it had all been for nothing.

Deacon's hands shook as he guided the drone back to the boat. The device touched down with a soft thud, a innocuous sound that belied the horror it had just witnessed. For a long moment, neither Billy or Deacon moved, the weight of their discovery pressing down on them like a physical force.

Billy was the first to break the silence, his voice barely above a whisper. "What the hell do we do now?"

Deacon shook his head, his eyes still fixed on the drone. "I don't know," he admitted, the words scraping his throat like shards of broken glass. "How do you prepare for something like this?"

He looked up, meeting Billy's gaze. The fear he saw there mirrored his own, amplifying it. "Everything we've done," Deacon continued, his voice hollow, "all the struggles, the sacrifices... it was all pointless."

Billy leaned back, running a hand through his hair. "Jesus, Deacon. We thought we were rebuilding. We thought we had a chance." He laughed, a harsh, bitter sound. "What a joke."

"All those people in Paradise," Deacon murmured, his mind racing through faces, names, lives that now seemed so fragile. "They have no idea what's coming."

The enormity of the task ahead began to sink in. It wasn't just about survival anymore. It was about facing an enemy that was evolving, strategizing, amassing in numbers they could barely comprehend.

"How do we even begin to fight this?" Billy asked, gesturing towards the shore where they now knew a myriad of cocoons lay hidden. "We're talking about almost a million of those things."

Deacon's jaw clenched. "I don't know if we can fight it," he admitted, the words feeling like a betrayal of everything he'd stood for. "Maybe... maybe all we can do is run."

The thought hung between them, heavy with implication. Running meant abandoning Paradise, abandoning the community they'd built, the people who relied on them.

"And go where?" Billy challenged, a spark of his old fire returning. "Where in this godforsaken world would be safe from that?"

Deacon had no answer. The hopelessness of their situation threatened to overwhelm him. He thought of Mary, of the future they'd tentatively begun to imagine together.

"We have to try," he said finally, his voice finding some strength. "Even if it's futile, even if we're just delaying the inevitable... we have to try."

"Do not go gentle into that good night. Rage, rage against the dying of the light," said Billy. "You know who said that?"

"Dylan Thomas," answered Deacon.

Billy shook his head. "No! It was my uncle Joe. Who the fuck is Dylan Thomas?"

Deacon laughed, but it was a laugh that almost broke his heart.

Billy smiled. He had been joking. He leaned in and hugged Deacon. "The world hasn't ended yet, kid." He ruffled Deacon's hair.

They fell into silence again, each lost in their own thoughts. The gentle lapping of waves against the boat's hull seemed obscene in the face of what they'd discovered, a reminder of a world that no longer existed.

Finally, Deacon reached for the boat's controls. "We should head back," he said, his voice heavy with the burden of what they carried. "They need to know. All of them."

As the engine sputtered to life, Deacon cast one last look at the naval base. From here, it looked peaceful, ordinary. But he knew the truth now, and that knowledge sat in his gut like a lead weight.

They turned the boat towards Paradise, leaving behind the visible world and heading towards an uncertain future. The struggle that lay ahead was immense, perhaps impossible. But it was all they had left.

As Paradise's shoreline appeared on the horizon, Deacon steeled himself for the task ahead. They carried with them not just information, but the death of hope, the end of the world as they knew it. And somehow, they had to find the strength to face it.

Billy ran his fingers through his hair in what looked to Deacon like a sign of intense stress. "You know some people are already wary of your ability, Deacon. This...this is going to be hard for many to swallow, but we have the footage. I just don't know if the community can handle this."

Deacon sighed, running a hand through his hair, unconsciously mimicking Billy's motion. "I know. But we can't keep it to ourselves. The threat is real; the whole community has a right to know about it."

Billy nodded grimly. "We'll start with the Professor and Amanda. Maybe they can help us figure out how to break it to the others."

"Billy," he said softly, "what if they think I'm somehow working with the horde? You heard what people have been saying, that I am spying for the growlers."

Billy placed a reassuring hand on Deacon's shoulder. "We'll figure this out together, kid."

"People in groups can be morons, right?" said Deacon. *That was what he was trying to explain to me. There's no predicting what morons will do. Groups don't reason the way individuals do.*

Deacon nodded, trying to draw strength from Billy's confidence. He took a deep breath, steeling himself for the challenges ahead. Whatever doubts or fears the community might have, Deacon knew one thing for certain: Paradise was not prepared for what was coming, and there was nothing Paradise *could* do to prepare; the odds were hopeless.

Chapter

The Resurrection of Nathanial

Billy Receives Shocking News

Billy leaned back in his chair, the weight of recent events pressing down on him like a physical force. The revelation of the mega horde in Alameda had sent shockwaves through Paradise. He could see it in the worried glances, hear it in the hushed conversations that fell silent when he approached. Fear was spreading, and Billy wasn't sure how to contain it. He thought about the Professor holed up in his lab, desperately searching for answers.

Maybe there simply are no answers. Maybe this time, we just have to run away. What would the community decide to do? Stand and fight against impossible odds? Flee and abandon everything they'd built? Billy shook his head, pushing the thoughts aside. Right now, his job was to man the communications center and wait for word from their eyes inside the cult.

It had been four weeks since Cassie had rejoined the cult, and there had been no word. Perhaps something terrible had happened to her. Billy had seen Amanda fretting about it. She had argued with the Professor about letting Cassie go.

Even Deacon was wandering around muttering and avoiding eye contact, though Billy thought that might be normal teenage boy behavior.

Billy's fingers drummed an anxious rhythm on the communications console; his eyes fixed on the softly glowing dials. The room hummed with the low buzz of electronics, punctuated by the occasional static crackle from the radio. He glanced at his watch for the hundredth time. He had agreed to take a shift, but there were a hundred tasks he'd rather be doing. He'd rather be scavenging for food, getting ammo, or even fishing.

This is stupid. If she hasn't contacted us by now, then she's probably dead. We made a terrible mistake sending Cassie back into the lion's den. He hated the thought of her being discovered, trying to relay information to Paradise. *What if she didn't even make it there? There are so many growlers around—*

Sven burst into the room. "You need to talk to Deacon. He respects you."

Oh shit, what has the kid done now?

Billy took a deep breath, ready to try and resolve whatever issue had come up. "What's going on?"

"Deacon and Mary keep trying to get time alone, and you know what that means." Sven stared at Billy.

Billy sighed. "They're young, dumb, and full of cum."

Sven shook his head in disgust. "I know it's all perfectly natural urges, but I am losing my mind with worry. There's a reason why, since ancient times, society created all these restrictions around sex. If she gets pregnant, her chances of survival plummet. How many mothers with babies have you seen lately? Not many. It's hard out there."

Billy shook his head. "Can't you talk to Mary? You're her father."

Sven shook her head. "I never used to need to be strict with her. She was always respectful, did her chores, tidied her room, worked hard at school. But suddenly, her hormones have kicked in, and I swear she is … she is." He stopped.

Billy smiled. "She is a teenage girl. You need to be firm. She needs your guidance."

Sven nodded, then shook his head, then nodded again. "I swear if I catch them together alone again, I will beat that boy within an inch of his life."

For a moment, the humor of the moment disappeared as Billy assessed Sven's words. He realized that Sven was not serious. He was protective, but Sven understood that Deacon was just being a teenage boy.

Sven shook his head. "I didn't mean that. I just don't know what else I can do. I can't lock her up. I can't keep an eye on her all the time. They are going to have sex sooner or later. Billy, Deacon respects you. You have a close relationship. Can you talk to the boy?"

“I have,” said Billy and then looked at Sven askance. “You know… I did get something in the market…” Billy rummaged in a draw and brought a strip of four condoms. “You can’t believe what they’re charging for them.”

Sven stared at them.

“I could give one to Deacon,” said Billy.

Sven kept staring at them, his face reddening. He began to pant in anger.

The radio suddenly burst to life, startling Billy from the conversation. He fumbled with the headset, heart racing as he heard Cassie's hushed voice emerge from the static.

"Paradise, this is Mockingbird. Do you copy?"

"Loud and clear, Mockingbird," Billy replied, relief washing over him. "Go ahead with your report."

Cassie's words tumbled out in a rushed whisper. "Reintegration successful. They bought my story hook, line, and sinker. I'm in. But I ain't staying. I’m heading back to Paradise. Shit’s going down here."

Billy allowed himself a small sigh of relief. Cassie was safe; they hadn’t got her killed. "Excellent work. What's the situation?"

"It's...intense," Cassie continued. "There was a horde attack a week ago. Small one, maybe a thousand growlers. But Billy, you should have seen how they handled it. It was like watching a well-oiled machine."

Billy's brow furrowed as he scribbled notes. "How so?"

"Military precision. They had it contained within minutes. New defensive structures, coordinated response teams. It's like they've leveled up in the past few months since I left them."

A cold knot formed in Billy's stomach. If the cult had improved this much in such a short time, what else were they capable of?

"There's more," Cassie's voice took on an urgent edge that made Billy sit up straighter. "During the attack, something...impossible happened."

"What do you mean, impossible?"

"A cocoon," Cassie said, her voice barely above a whisper now. "They just deposited it in the middle of the fight. And when it opened..."

Billy leaned in, hanging on her every word.

"It was Nathanial, the President's son, the leader of the cult here in California. Alive. Unharmed."

The pencil slipped from Billy's fingers, clattering to the floor. "That's not possible...the way he was being chased by a horde of sprinting growlers. I can't understand how he could possibly have escaped."

"I know what I saw, Billy," Cassie insisted. "It was him. And he's...different. The way he talks, the way he moves. It's like he's been reborn with some kind of new purpose."

Billy's mind reeled as he tried to process this information. "How are people reacting?"

"Like he's the second coming. You should see how quickly he's consolidating power. The fanaticism is off the charts. He's spouting all this stuff about divine resurrection and a holy war against the unbelievers. People are eating it up."

A cold dread settled in the pit of Billy's stomach, spreading outward until his entire body felt numb. *How is the Professor's science going to explain this?*

"They are having purges of those deemed not fanatical enough. They are continually talking about marching to the Paradise community to teach you guys a lesson. Billy, it is really dangerous here. I have to go," Cassie's voice suddenly became urgent. "I am returning to Paradise. I will be there as soon as I can. I am not staying in this shit show. You guys need to prepare."

The radio went dead, leaving Billy in stunned silence. He stared at his hastily scrawled notes, the implications of what he'd just heard crashing over him like a tidal wave.

Nathanial was alive.

The cult was stronger than ever.

And they were coming.

Billy shot to his feet, nearly knocking over his chair in his haste. He had to tell the others. They needed to prepare, to fortify their defenses, to—

When the community finds out about this, they're going to panic; they'll fall apart. But who am I to deny them this information?

Chapter

PARADISE DIVIDED

Mary Supporting Deacon

Deacon instinctively wiped the sweat from his brow with his forearm as he entered the market clearing of Paradise.

I miss air conditioning, he thought. His mind was suddenly flooded with the feeling of home with its central HVAC, soft couch, fridge with ice and filtered cold water, and sparkling pool with a little waterfall. *Oh, I'd love to be in that pool right now, standing under the waterfall, preferably with Mary.* He built a mental image of Mary in a bathing suit, and he had to stop walking so he could breathe and relax for a moment.

And I miss Mom and Dad, he thought as he continued to walk. He often wondered where they were and what they were doing. Were they looking for him? Or were they just trying to survive, like he was? *Perhaps one day, I can enter Oakland and check my home. Mom might have tried to leave a message there. Dad…* His father had been on a business trip in Singapore when the outbreak started. *There probably would not have been flights back to the U.S., so he might still be in Singapore. I wonder if there are growlers there.*

He felt sadness grip his throat and his heart and squeeze until tears brimmed in his eyes. *Fuck that!* His internal voice berated himself. *I will not fall apart. I am not going to* … His mother's face appeared before him.

He remembered her voice, "Come on, do your homework, and I'll take you to Nation's for a cheeseburger and a shake."

Grow up! He told himself. *She's probably dead. She probably died the first day. You need to stop feeling things and get back to surviving.*

He tripped over a tent rope and tumbled to the floor. *Ugh!* When he stood, he was so frustrated that he punched the tent canvas, which had no resistance, making him lose his balance and fall again. Stupid! Lying on the floor, he giggled, and then he burst into tears for just a second before stifling them.

I WILL NOT FALL APART!

Whoa! Emotional roller coaster. I'm too old to miss my parents, and I'm too smart to be punching inanimate objects. With a groan, he stood and brushed the dirt off his clothes. *I really need to launder my clothes. It's been months; I must be ripe.* He remembered his father hugging him at the airport, the smell of his freshly laundered shirt. Deacon had been impatient and embarrassed to hug in public and pushed his father away. *If only I'd known that was the last time I would ever see him.*

STOP THINKING OF SAD THINGS!

"I can't fall apart," he whispered to the air.

He was on his way to the sprawling tent that served as Paradise's makeshift community hall. People wanted to discuss all the bad news that Paradise had received. His stomach churned with a potent mixture of hunger, dread, and determination. He paused at the entrance, taking a deep breath to steel himself for what lay ahead. The murmur of voices from within sounded like the angry buzz of disturbed hornets.

He pushed through the heavy canvas flap, the heat and noise hitting him like a physical force. The tent was packed, bodies pressed close in the stifling air. Deacon's eyes swept across the crowd, noting the clear divisions that had formed. It was as if an invisible line had been drawn, separating those who still believed in him from those who saw him as a threat. Ever since he had explained what the voice in Alameda had said, some people thought he created the bad news rather than just delivered it.

Peter had called him a "banshee." A harbinger of death.

Snippets of hushed conversations reached his ears as he moved through the throng:

"Always bad news when that kid opens his mouth..."

"How does he really know what the horde is planning?"

"What if he's helping them without realizing it?"

"Why is it always him? Why does he always know?"

Each whispered accusation felt like a knife twisting in Deacon's gut. These were people he'd fought alongside, people he'd risked his life to protect. Now, their eyes followed him with suspicion, fear, even hatred. The weight of their mistrust pressed down on him, threatening to crush his resolve.

A flash of movement caught his eye, and suddenly Mary was there, her presence like a lifeline in a stormy sea. She grabbed his hand, squeezing it reassuringly as she led him toward a row of seats. As they sat, her hand found his thigh, the warmth of her touch a welcome comfort amid the hostility of the room's atmosphere. For a brief moment, Deacon allowed himself to relax, drawing strength from her unwavering support.

The respite was short-lived. With the speed and precision of a military maneuver, Sven materialized between them, his bulk effectively separating Deacon from Mary. The older man's eyes bored into Deacon, a clear warning in their steely gaze. Message received: stay away from my daughter.

Deacon's jaw clenched, frustration bubbling up inside him. He was trying to save them all, and this was how they treated him? Like some kind of pariah? Like a child who couldn't be trusted? He opened his mouth, ready to voice his indignation, but Billy's authoritative voice cut through the din, calling the meeting to order.

All eyes turned to the front as Billy activated the jury-rigged projector. "Some of you have not seen this," said Billy.

The drone footage of Alameda flickered to life on the makeshift screen, the images somehow more horrifying in the harsh light of day. Deacon watched the faces of the crowd, seeing his fear reflected at him a hundredfold. Gasps of shock gave way to muttered curses as the true scale of the threat became apparent.

When the footage ended, leaving them in oppressive silence, Billy nodded to Deacon. It was time. His legs felt like lead as he stood, his heart pounding so loudly he was sure everyone must hear it. He cleared his throat, acutely aware of every eye in the room fixed upon him.

"I know what you all just saw is terrifying," he began, his voice stronger than he felt. "But there's more. The Voice... I heard it again."

A ripple of unease passed through the crowd. Deacon pressed on, recounting what he'd heard about the horde's plans, their numbers, their intent. As he spoke, he watched the myriad of emotions play across the faces before him. Fear, yes, that was expected. Disbelief from some, their minds rebelling against the horrific reality. But it was the anger that caught him off guard. Anger directed not at the threat but at him, the messenger.

Some faces hardened with suspicion, eyes narrowing as if trying to peer into his very thoughts. Deacon felt exposed and vulnerable. Did they think he was lying? Or worse, that he was somehow complicit in this nightmare?

As he finished speaking, the Professor stepped forward, a sheaf of papers in his hand. "We have additional threats," he announced, his academic tone a jarring contrast to the tension in the room. "Our inside source, in the cult, has sent a report. The cult, with Nathanial back as leader, is planning to attack."

Deacon could feel the fear in the room, a living, breathing thing that threatened to suffocate them all.

Billy moved to the center, his face grim as he laid out the stark reality of their situation. "Let's be clear about what we're facing," he said, his voice cutting through the murmurs. "The cult has 7,500 trained soldiers and a battalion of tanks. The horde is a million-strong. We have 75 surviving trained soldiers, 1500 men and 800 women, plus almost 300 children." He paused, letting the numbers sink in. "And the voice...it didn't work last time we tried it."

The Professor cleared his throat. "Our scavenging raids have actually lowered our ammunition reserves. We have 17,000 rounds for the next fight. It is nowhere near enough."

As the Professor finished, the tent fell into a silence so profound that Deacon became aware of the sound of his own breathing. For a moment, it was as if everyone had forgotten how to breathe.

Then, like a dam breaking, the reactions began to ripple through the crowd.

A middle-aged woman slumped forward, her face buried in her hands, shoulders shaking with silent sobs. Beside her, a man stared blankly at the floor, his eyes unfocused, mouth slightly agape as if he'd forgotten how to close it.

To Deacon's left, an older couple clutched each other's hands so tightly their knuckles had turned white. The woman's lips moved in what might have been a prayer, though no sound escaped her.

Near the back, a young man suddenly stood, kicking his chair backwards with a clatter that echoed through the tent. Without a word, he stormed out, the canvas flap slapping shut behind him.

Deacon's eyes found Mary, who was so often the sole source of optimism, but now, she sat rigid, her face pale, eyes wide with a fear she was clearly fighting to control. Sven, next to her, had his head bowed, one large hand covering his eyes.

The Professor fumbled with his papers, dropping several to the floor. As he bent to retrieve them, Deacon noticed his hands were shaking.

A low murmur began to build, fragmented whispers growing in volume and urgency:

"We're all going to die."

"What's the point of fighting?"

"Maybe we should just... give up."

Billy tried to call for order, but his voice lacked its usual authority. It was swallowed up by the growing tide of despair that swept through the tent.

Deacon watched the transformation happening before his eyes. The determined survivors who had fought so hard, for so long, were crumbling. Hope, that fragile thing they'd clung to through every hardship, was visibly seeping away, leaving behind hollow-eyed shells of the people he knew.

And in some faces, he saw something that chilled him more than any growler ever had: a cold, empty acceptance. The look of those who had already given up.

The realization hit Deacon like a physical blow. This was how it ended. Not with a bloody battle, but with a room full of people quietly deciding that the fight was no longer winnable.

Maybe we should have lied to them. Maybe we should have sugar-coated the truth. People with zero hope don't even fight. He tried to think of something positive to say. Something thread of hope.

It was Peter who broke the silence, his voice booming across the tent. "This is Deacon's fault!" he shouted, jabbing a meaty finger in Deacon's direction. "He sent that drone in without consulting us. He's probably the reason the horde wants to attack!"

A chorus of agreement rose from Peter's supporters, the accusation seeming to release a floodgate of pent-up fear and anger. Deacon felt as if he'd been physically struck, the force of their hatred staggering him.

Peter, emboldened by the support, pressed on. "Our leadership is too weak," he continued, his voice rising. We've given people like him too much freedom, and look where it's gotten us! We need strong leadership and decisive action!"

The implication was clear, and it sent a chill down Deacon's spine. He'd seen firsthand what happened when fear drove people to embrace authoritarian leaders. The cult was proof of how quickly things could go wrong.

"We don't need dictators!" Deacon shouted back, surprising himself with the force of his own voice. "That's exactly what we've been fighting against!"

Peter's eyes flashed dangerously, a cruel smile twisting his lips. "Child, sit down and let the adults try to fix the problem you've created."

The dismissal stung, stoking the fire of Deacon's anger. "I didn't create the problem," he retorted, his voice cracking with emotion. "I just brought it to your attention! Would you rather be blind to the danger?"

The Professor interjected, his calm voice a stark contrast to the heated exchange. "Let's not forget that Deacon was the hero who saved Paradise with his ingenious use of the recording of the voice."

Peter wasn't backing down. He turned to Deacon, challenge written across his face. "Okay, Deacon, big shot. Do you have a plan to save us? Do you know how we defeat this threat?"

Deacon opened his mouth, then closed it, words failing him. He had warnings, yes, but solutions? The magnitude of the problem overwhelmed him, and all he had was self-doubt.

Peter nodded grimly, taking Deacon's silence as confirmation. "Well, I have a solution," he announced. "We beg the cult to return, and we pledge them fealty and faith. It's our only chance at survival. They have a fully armed division and tanks."

The words hit Deacon like a bucket of ice water, shocking him out of his spiral of self-doubt. "Are you insane?" he shouted, finding his voice again. "The cult will take terrible vengeance. Only the young women would be allowed to live, to service their perverted leadership!"

He looked around the room, locking eyes with the women and girls in the crowd. "Is that the future you want? To be slaves to those monsters?"

Peter sneered, undeterred. "Well, you don't have a better plan, do you? Sometimes, survival means making hard choices. What's your brilliant solution, boy?"

The silence stretched, thick and oppressive. Deacon felt the weight of every eye in the room on him, a mix of hope and skepticism on their faces. His mind raced, grasping for an answer, any answer that could save them from this nightmare. Then, almost surprising himself, the solution crystallized in his mind. It was so obvious; he couldn't believe he hadn't thought of it sooner.

"Actually, I do have a plan," he said, his voice growing stronger with each word.

The room fell silent, all attention focused on him. Even Peter looked taken aback, clearly not expecting this turn of events.

"Isn't it obvious?" Deacon continued, his confidence growing as he spoke. He glared at Peter, daring him to answer. "Given these odds, we can't win a direct confrontation. We need to run away. Make a new community somewhere the hunting is good, somewhere more defensible. We have the skills, we have the determination. We can start over somewhere the horde and the cult can't find us."

A murmur ran through the crowd, a mix of hope and skepticism. Deacon could see his words landing, see people considering the possibility.

But Peter wasn't done. He scoffed loudly, drawing attention back to himself. "And the cult and horde will just let us go, will they? They'll wave goodbye as we pack up and leave? Don't be naive, boy. There's nowhere we can run that they won't follow."

The room erupted into chaos, the tenuous thread of hope Deacon had offered, fraying under the weight of fear and doubt. Accusations flew, and tempers flared. Deacon watched in dismay as the community he'd fought so hard to protect tore itself apart from within. All he could hear was indictments and panic.

"We'd be foolish to listen to a child."

"We can't trust him!"

"But what choice do we have?"

"The cult will kill us all!"

"At least with the cult, we have a chance!"

"He should never have used that drone!"

The cacophony of voices blended into a roar. Deacon felt overwhelmed, the weight of their expectations, their fear, their mistrust threatening to crush him. The sound of the crowd reminded him of the voice within the growlers, and he realized that crowds of people actually do have a group mind, but their intelligence hides it, sometimes, but not at times like this. The mob felt fear. The mob was paranoid. The groupthink was toxic.

The mob was not looking at him anymore; now, they were arguing with each other. The vehemence and ugliness of it tore at his heart.

He caught Mary's eye and saw the worry etched on her face. Sven stood between them, a physical manifestation of the gulf that seemed to keep them apart forever. Mary pushed her father aside, moved forward, and put her arms around Deacon.

Oh, that feels wonderful.

In that moment, he realized, for the first time, that his feelings for Mary had been nothing but sexual since he had met her, but suddenly, there was something else. He realized she was actually a good, caring person and that he had been so caught up in her physical beauty and her willingness to share her body with him that he had not actually connected with her until now.

A feeling swept over him. It was like coming out of a cold shower and being wrapped in a warm towel. He clenched his eyes shut and kept them closed. This was an emotional roller coaster he wanted to embrace.

She has always been good and caring, but my hormones were just focused on one thing. A feeling of shame also flooded him. *I have not treated her right. I have not bared my soul to her, but she has feelings for me.*

He could hear the mob beginning to quieten and he heard them leaving, with no clear decision made.

He opened his eyes and saw Sven, but this time, his expression was not angry. Sven looked thoughtful and sad, and he gave a sigh and a nod.

Deacon felt a leaden weight settle in his chest. The division within the community was as dangerous as any external threat. Perhaps more so. They had survived the horde before, survived the cult's oppression, but this...how could they fight an enemy that lived in their own hearts?

He and Mary remained rooted to the spot. They were facing impossible odds from without and now fracturing from within. How could they possibly survive this?

I may have been falling apart, but with Mary, I know that we will find a way to survive. Mary can't die. Mary can't become a cult plaything. Mary can't become a growler. Whatever it takes, I will keep her safe.

He had found strength.

Chapter

SAMANTHA'S DILEMMA

Deacon and Samantha run into Trouble

The woods were eerily quiet, save for the occasional rustle of leaves in the wind. Samantha crouched low beside Deacon, her eyes constantly scanning the tree line for any sign of movement. Growler activity had been quiet for a while, but the quiet itself put her on edge.

The community was desperate for food, and Deacon had put all his faith into this rabbit-catching idea, but something about it felt too easy—too hopeful. And hope was a dangerous thing these days. She knew he was a bookworm who had not been very outdoorsy prior to the outbreak.

"Are you sure this will work, kid?" she whispered, keeping her voice low to avoid spooking any wildlife—or attracting anything worse. She watched him closely, hoping for a flicker of doubt, something to tell her that he wasn't so certain either.

But Deacon just smiled and shrugged. His eyes, sharp and determined, remained focused on the burrows in front of them. "It'll work," he whispered back, his tone more hopeful than confident. "The smoke will drive them out. The nets will do the rest." It sounded like he was trying to convince himself. "It worked in the book I read."

She bit back a sigh. Deacon was a good kid—smart, resourceful—but he was too young. One day, he'd be a fine man once he had learned some wisdom. He needed more time to learn life's lessons. The world had taken too much from him already, and she knew he was trying to prove himself, not just to her but to everyone. She wanted to believe in him. But the constant gnawing at the back of her mind—the voice that warned her something would always go wrong—wouldn't let her.

Still, she had no choice. They needed food. The community was beginning to starve. Deacon needed a win. If he could bring a new food source to the community, then maybe they would rally around him again, and she couldn't take that from him. Not after everything. Not when she saw how hard he was trying to be useful, how hard he worked to be something more than a lost, scared boy.

She kept her doubts to herself, not wanting to dampen his enthusiasm. He'd been through enough, and the last thing he needed was her second-guessing him. "Okay," she muttered. "Let's light it up."

Deacon struck the lighter against the kindling. As soon as the smoke began to rise from the bundle of dry brush, curling toward the warren's entrances, Samantha stood back. The smoke billowed, swirling lazily through the air, finding its way into the narrow burrows, and within minutes, they could hear the frantic scuffling of rabbits.

Oh wow, maybe this will work after all.

"Come on," Deacon muttered under his breath, his knuckles white on his clenched fists. He walked over to where they had staked the nets.

A minute passed and then another. Samantha was about to voice her concern when suddenly, a rabbit darted out, fast and terrified. It ran down the long netting until it got thoroughly tangled.

"Okay, kill it," said Samantha.

Deacon looked at it, and his mouth dropped open. "Oh, but it's so cute."

Samantha stared at him.

"Just kidding," he said. "We need to eat, and it is food, but we have to wait until the nets are full. Then, I'll kill, skin, and gut them. There were illustrations in the book. It'll be easy."

More rabbits emerged from the warren. Deacon smiled. Soon, the nets were full, wriggling with panicked creatures.

Samantha let out a slow breath of relief. *Maybe the kid had been right after all.* Deacon's eyes lit up as the pile grew. "Gate tax will take half of them for the community, but we'll have enough to feed ourselves for days," he said, his voice full of that rare, youthful excitement that had all but disappeared since the world had fallen apart.

She couldn't help but smile just a little. He deserved this moment. "You did good," she said, her voice soft. She didn't hand out praise often, but Deacon needed to hear it.

But as soon as the words left her mouth, a sound in the distance sent a chill down her spine—a low, guttural growl that was all too familiar. Her heart sank. Of course. Nothing ever went smoothly anymore.

"Shit," she hissed, eyes darting to the trees. The growlers were coming. She could already hear them, shuffling through the underbrush, drawn by the smoke and the noise.

Deacon froze, his face draining of color. He grabbed the net and tied the end. "We need to move," he said, his voice trying to be strong but cracking just slightly.

The net now acted as a bag, which he slung over his shoulder. He had his ax in one hand and stood between her and the direction of the growling.

She almost laughed at the sight of him trying to protect her. He had heart, no doubt about that, but this was no time for heroics. "Stay close," she barked, pulling her bow from her back and notching an arrow. She and Deacon both had guns, but they would be a last resort.

The first growler stumbled out of the tree line, its sunken, milky eyes locking onto them. Deacon moved fast, slamming his ax into its forehead. His movements were quick and precise, but more were coming and fast.

"Focus!" she called out as she loosed an arrow, striking another growler through the eye. The creature crumpled to the ground. "There's too many!"

Deacon was breathing hard, but he didn't stop. He stabbed, slashed, and dodged with everything he had, but she could see the exhaustion setting in. It wasn't the physical toll—it was the mental strain, the fear gnawing at him with every strike.

She loosed six more arrows, taking down four growlers, but then she had no more left. She stepped in front of Deacon, withdrew her hammer, and took down two more growlers with quick, practiced blows. Her arms burned, but she didn't slow down. "Stay behind me," she ordered her voice hard.

Of course, he did not obey. Three more growlers emerged from a thick tangle of branches. He took down two of them while she handled the third.

They stood side by side, waiting for the next attack, but there was silence. After a few minutes, she realized it was over.

"That could've been worse," she muttered, not looking at him. She didn't want him to see the worry etched on her face.

Deacon nodded, his voice shaky. "Yeah. Let's just get the rabbits back to Paradise."

Samantha nodded. This wasn't the first time they'd had to fight off growlers, but something about this one felt different. Maybe it was the way Deacon had thrown himself into the fight, trying so hard to be brave. Or maybe it was the sinking feeling in her gut that told her the worst was yet to come.

The guards at the community's gates eagerly took half of the rabbits as the tax for the general fund. Samantha felt a small wave of relief as they stepped inside, but it was fleeting.

A crowd had gathered near the entrance, their faces a mix of curiosity and suspicion. At the center of it all stood Peter, arms crossed, his expression smug and self-satisfied. Samantha's jaw tightened. She'd had enough run-ins with Peter to know he was trouble. The kind of trouble that could tear a group apart from the inside.

The moment he saw her, his sneer deepened. "Well, look who decided to come back," Peter called out, his voice carrying over the murmurs of the crowd. "Did you have fun playing with the growlers out there?"

Samantha shot him a sharp look, but she held her tongue. She didn't have the energy for this right now. They had food, and that should have been enough.

But Peter wasn't going to let it go. He never did.

"The smoke," he continued, his voice rising with every word, "you think that didn't attract every growler in the area? Are you trying to get us all killed?"

A murmur rippled through the crowd. Some nodded in agreement, and others looked away. Samantha could feel the weight of their eyes on her, and it made her stomach turn.

"We brought back a couple of dozen rabbits," Samantha said, keeping her voice steady. "That smoke drew the rabbits out. We dealt with the growlers."

Peter scoffed, stepping forward. "It's not just the growlers, is it? It's the cult. They're out there, watching, waiting for their chance to come and get you because you killed their prophet. And we are all just going to be collateral damage."

Her chest tightened. "They don't need the smoke to know where we are. We evicted their perverted asses from here."

"Yeah, and do you think they'll ever stop hunting us while you're here?" Peter's voice was venomous, dripping with self-righteousness. "You killed their prophet. They want you dead, and they'll keep coming until they get what they want. You put us all in danger just by existing."

She clenched her fists at her sides, fighting the urge to lash out. She had done what she had to do. Killing the cult's prophet had been necessary. She had no regrets about that, but Peter, with his smug arrogance, was twisting it all, making her out to be the problem, and the worst part was, she could see the doubt in the crowd, see how easily they could be swayed.

Why is he doing this, she wondered.

"They'll come for all of us," Peter continued, his voice rising to a fevered pitch. "Unless we give them what they want. Unless we hand her over."

Samantha's heart skipped a beat. Was he serious? Was he actually suggesting they turn her over to the cult? She glanced around at the faces in the crowd, trying to gauge their reaction. Some looked horrified, but others—others were nodding, considering the possibility.

Her stomach churned.

"You really think they'd spare you?" Samantha asked, her voice low and even. She forced herself to stay calm, though every muscle in her body screamed for her to fight back. "You think the cult cares about peace? They want control. They'll only keep you alive if you serve their purposes, either as slaves in their fields or youngsters for their harems."

Samantha's words hung in the air, but the crowd seemed split. She could see the doubt flickering in their eyes. Fear did that to people—it made them forget logic, forget loyalty. In the face of danger, they'd grasp at any hope, no matter how false or short-lived.

Peter seized on that uncertainty. "Maybe they want control," he said, "but without you here, we'd stand a better chance of making a deal. We're not the ones who killed their leader. You are." His gaze swept the crowd. "She's more trouble than she's worth. The cult won't stop, and the growlers won't either. How many more lives will we risk because of her?"

The murmurs grew louder. Samantha's jaw tightened. She'd been through worse than this. She'd faced down death more times than she could count, but betrayal—this? This was something she hadn't prepared for. Not from her own people.

She glanced at Deacon, who stood just to her right, still as a statue, his face pale but his eyes burning with defiance. The kid had been through hell, and now this. She wanted to tell him it'd be fine, that the community wouldn't turn on them—but even she didn't believe that anymore.

Deacon's fists were clenched. "They won't spare us," he said, addressing the crowd now. "The cult isn't interested in deals. They want control, and if you think handing Samantha over will stop them, you're wrong. It'll embolden them. They'll keep coming for you. They'll take back Paradise, and when that happens, you'll have no one left to fight for you."

A silence fell over the group. Samantha could see some of them wavering, torn between reason and fear.

Peter wasn't finished. "Bullshit," he said. "Some of us lived in peace with the cult before your lot came and picked a fight." He turned his back on Samantha to address the growing crowd. "What other choice do we really have, huh? We can't keep running from both the cult and the growlers, not when they outnumber us so much. Before Samantha and her band of troublemakers came here, we had the cult and the army on our side. Our ammunition was in the millions. We had helicopters, machine guns, RPGs. Now we're down to a few hundred guns and a few thousand bullets. Under the cult, we had containers of food arriving; now we starve."

Samantha felt her face flush with rage. "If it wasn't for Deacon and…"

"Oh, I know!" shouted Peter, interrupting her. "You claim Deacon saved us with his voice trick. Well, I claim bullshit. Bull…shit! What I think happened is this. The growlers stopped of their own accord, for their own demonic reasons, and then this little brat"—he whacked Deacon on the side of the head—"made up the voice to claim credit for the victory."

"What the hell are you talking about?" shouted Deacon. "That's not true."

Peter shook his head slowly. "Oh, you are the big hero, aren't you? Or maybe you just wanted some attention. Maybe you just wanted to act like a hero and have people worship you. Well, I don't worship you! I think you're just a naughty little boy." He grabbed Peter by his neck. Maybe you need to be punished.

Samantha stepped to intervene but found her way blocked by a large man from the crowd. She tried to push past him, but he stood firm and held her away.

"Leave him alone; he's just a kid." She felt her voice crack with emotion. Deacon was 15 years old, but he looked like he was 12. She knew he had been considered a nerd at school. He had described to her how the jocks would surround him like redwoods surround shrubs. She reached for her knife, but as she withdrew it, the big man held her wrist and twisted it until the knife fell to the floor.

Peter took off his belt and, holding Deacon with one hand, prepared to beat him.

Samantha looked desperately at the crowd. Some of them were alarmed at the threat of violence against Deacon, others were nodding in agreement with it. She could not believe that anyone would stand by and allow the boy to be beaten.

Peter screamed. Deacon had bit him on the side of his stomach. "You little shit!" cried Peter lifting his shirt to show the bite wound. "You're nothing but a growler."

Deacon struggled to free himself but was wrestled to the floor.

Peter sat on his chest, snarling. He formed a fist.

He's going to beat the crap of the kid, thought Samantha. In desperation, she hurled herself at the man blocking her from intervening. She scratched and bit and yelled. The man easily lifted her and slammed her down with such violence she felt the air leave her lungs. She groaned, strained to breathe in.

She knew she was impossibly matched. The difference in strength between this big man and herself was insurmountable. *Why did God make men so much stronger,* she thought.

A shotgun blasted into the air. Nothing gets people's attention like a shotgun blast. She looked over and saw Sven standing with a calm but menacing expression.

"Get off the kid. Get off, woman." Sven pumped the gun.

Billy, Carl, Amanda, and the Professor ran up behind Sven. They all had weapons drawn.

There was a long silence in which Samantha got to her feet and gasped in some breaths.

She stepped forward, her voice croaky but somehow commanding. "I know you're scared," she said, her gaze sweeping over the faces of the community. "I am too. But I've fought for this community since day one, and I'm not going to stop now. We have a chance—together—to survive. We can't let fear tear us apart because once that happens, we've already lost."

Her words seemed to hang in the air, the crowd shifting uneasily. For a moment, no one spoke. Peter's eyes narrowed, and she could tell he was calculating his next move, searching for another angle to sway them.

But before he could speak, Billy stepped forward. "Let me explain something," he said.

Samantha knew Billy was smart and, at times, quite eloquent, and she wondered what argument he would offer. To her surprise, he simply kicked Peter in the balls. It was one smooth, swift motion that connected with so much power that even Samantha winced.

Peter fell to the floor, grabbing his groin.

"Explanation over." Billy picked Deacon up, brushed the dirt off the boy's jeans, and they walked away with Samantha hurrying to catch up.

She looked back and saw Peter rolling on the ground. A smile spread on her face. "Nice explanation, Billy."

The crowd dispersed slowly, some casting glances at her, others at Peter. Samantha knew this wasn't over, not by a long shot. The community had been divided tonight. She could feel the crack that Peter had created. It would only take one more push to shatter it completely.

As the people drifted away, Deacon remained at her side, silent but steady. She looked down at him, and for a moment, the weight of everything pressed in on her. She had her own doubts and her own fears, but seeing the resolve in his eyes gave her the strength to push them aside.

"You did good, kid," she said softly, her voice barely above a whisper. "Real good."

Deacon gave a small nod, but the tension in his face hadn't eased. "They'll come for you," he said quietly. "Peter's friends, I mean."

Samantha glanced around, making sure no one was listening. "I know," she admitted, her voice grim. "But we'll be ready."

They had to be. Because if there was one thing she'd learned in this world, it was that survival wasn't just about looking out for growlers—it was about looking out for the darkness inside people too.

Chapter

THE VIPER'S NEST

Cassie and Peter

Inside Peter's container, Cassie stood before her gathered followers, her stance confident and her eyes gleaming with malicious triumph. The dim light cast sinister shadows across her face, accentuating the cruel curve of her lips.

"Well done, Peter," she purred, her voice dripping with praise. "Your efforts to turn the community against Samantha and Deacon have been most effective. They're now seen as too dangerous to keep around, just as I planned."

Peter stood in obvious pain from his groin, but he preened under her approval. He smiled and then winced.

Cassie's expression hardened, her voice taking on a razor's edge. "But now, it's time to move on to the next phase. Paradise has outlived its usefulness. Within the next 24 hours, we will destroy it, once and for all."

A ripple of excitement passed through the group, their eyes gleaming with anticipation. They had long awaited this moment, the chance to strike a decisive blow against those who had unwittingly sheltered them.

"Here's what we're going to do," Cassie continued, her tone brooking no argument. "I will persuade Samantha and the Professor's group that it's no longer safe here. They'll offer to take those who are loyal to them to the bunker. Once they've shown us the secret entrance and we've gained access to the armory and the lab, we'll execute them all."

She paused, a wicked smile playing on her lips. "Except, perhaps, for the Professor and Deacon. They may still prove useful to our cause. And Samantha...her death will be recorded. A little gift for our friends in the cult, to curry their favor. They're still a useful force, after all."

Cassie's gaze swept over the assembled group, lingering on Peter. "You and a few others will stay behind, Peter. Make a show of opposing me to allay any suspicions. The rest of you, prepare for the journey. We leave at dawn."

One of the followers looked confused.

"Something unclear?" Cassie asked.

The follower looked alarmed. "I…I just don't understand how that ends Paradise."

"Well, once Samantha escapes, then Peter can persuade the remnants here that it is time to leave to escape the wrath of the cult with their"—she chuckled—"battalion of tanks." She paused. "Alright, let's be about our tasks, shall we."

As the others filed out, Cassie crooked a finger at Peter, a sultry look in her eyes. "Not you, Peter. I have another task for you."

Peter swallowed hard and looked nervous as he approached her. Cassie's hand snaked out, grabbing his collar and pulling him close.

"Oh, I don't know if I can," he said. "I'm still in pain."

"I need servicing again," she breathed, her lips brushing his ear. "I know you're bruised down there, and I am not going to be kind or gentle with you."

Peter looked miserable.

"However, I don't care how much pain you're in; I expect your performance to be excellent as usual. You start when I say start. You do not flag or fail. You finish exactly when I tell you to." She smiled at him. She cupped his face with her hands. "I want you to be rougher with me. Even rougher than usual. I need to look at the part of the victim when we reach the bunker. Use your belt. Use your fists. Use your imagination. I need you to be an animal."

Peter's brow furrowed, confusion and unease warring in his eyes. "But why? Surely there's no need for..."

Cassie's eyes flashed dangerously, her grip on his collar tightening. "Are you questioning me, Peter?"

Peter blanched, quickly shaking his head. "No, of course not. I just..."

"It's not just a matter of need," Cassie snapped, her nails digging into his skin. "It's a matter of want. And what I want, I get. Do you understand?"

Peter nodded frantically. "Yes, Mistress Cassie. I understand."

A slow, predatory smile spread across Cassie's face. "Good. Now, let's get started, shall we? And remember, Peter...no permanent damage, but I want to see bruises. I want to feel the pain. And once I say go, there are no safe words. Make this convincing."

As Peter set to his grim task, Cassie's mind raced with visions of the destruction to come. Paradise would fall, and from its ashes, she would rise—the unquestioned ruler of a world reborn in her image.

She understood her own psychology. She understood why she needed to be hurt. It was the only way she could be free.

Peter punched her in the face and pushed her violently down. He held a gag up in front of her eyes. The gag was what thrilled her the most. Once gagged, she could not order him. That way, she knew whatever perversion he surprised with came from his own psyche, from his own desires. What he did within the limits she had set came from the demons in his inner id, deep within his ego.

He was her puppet, but in these moments, she knew she was the focus of the beast that lay within all men. The fact that he, too, was in pain somehow made everything even more delicious.

The doctors were right about me, she mused. *No amount of therapy in the world can fix me.*

Peter put on a glove with spikes on the knuckles. "First, I beat you with it, then it goes inside you."

Oh, you lovely boy.

She knew this was going to be the most painful and most pleasurable session of her life. Afterward, she would destroy Paradise, take over the bunker, and kill Samantha and her friends.

Good times. Good times.

Chapter

MIDNIGHT WARNING

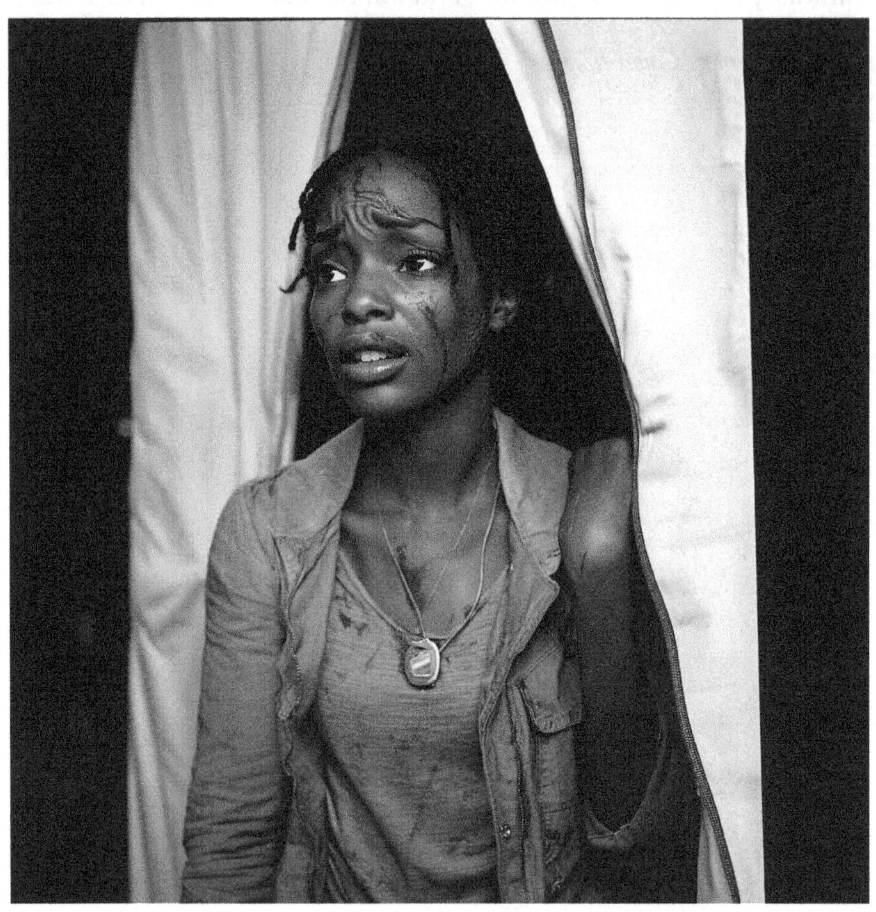

Cassie the Victim

The infirmary was bathed in the soft glow of battery-powered lanterns, casting eerie shadows across the makeshift beds. Amanda stifled a yawn as she reorganized the dwindling medical supplies. She rattled the pain medicine bottle. Only three pills remained. There was plenty of alcohol and laundered bandages. She had a little clove oil and some prenatal vitamins.

Night duty was always a challenge, but lately, it felt like a Herculean task. The weight of Paradise's precarious situation pressed down on her, making each hour feel like an eternity.

Willow bark, she thought—*its salicin could ease the throbbing headaches and joint pain that is all too common right now. And there's California poppy, blooming in bright patches in many areas; I know I can use its leaves to make a mild sedative. Yarrow might help, too, especially for wounds and inflammation.*

She sighed. *I took modern medicine for granted. What I would give for a fully stocked pharmacy right now.*

A sudden commotion at the entrance snapped her to attention. Amanda's eyes widened as she saw Cassie stumble in, her appearance a far cry from the composed woman who had left for her dangerous mission. Cassie's clothes were torn and dirty, her hair a tangled mess, and her eyes wild with a mixture of fear and urgency.

"Cassie?" Amanda rushed forward, catching the woman as she swayed on her feet. "What happened?"

Cassie gripped Amanda's arms, her fingers digging in with desperate strength. "No time," she gasped. "Amanda, you have to listen. The cult...they're coming. Now."

Amanda felt a chill run down her spine. "Slow down," she said, guiding Cassie to a nearby cot. "Take a deep breath and tell me everything."

As Cassie sank onto the cot, Amanda's trained eye quickly cataloged her visible injuries. Bruises mottled her arms, and there was a stiffness to her movements that suggested hidden injuries.

"As I was leaving," Cassie began, her voice trembling, "I overheard them. The cult is mobilizing. They'll be here in a couple of days, maybe less."

Amanda's heart raced, but she forced herself to remain calm. "Okay, we knew they might be coming. We can prepare—"

"No, you don't understand," Cassie interrupted, her eyes locking onto Amanda's with terrifying intensity. "There are traitors in Paradise. People who've been in contact with the cult. When they attack, there will be an assault from within as well."

The implications of Cassie's words hit Amanda like a physical blow. *Traitors? Within Paradise?* She realized, awful though it was, it made sense. Desperate people would be willing to betray in order to live. Then there was Peter and his followers. *Yeah, they'd be eager to make any deal they could.*

She gently helped Cassie remove her tattered shirt. What she saw made her gasp involuntarily. Angry red welts crisscrossed Cassie's back, unmistakably the result of a whipping.

"Oh, Cassie," Amanda breathed, horror and sympathy warring within her. "What did they do to you?"

Cassie flinched away from Amanda's touch, her face a mask of pain and something else...shame? "It's nothing," she muttered. "Just focus on what I'm telling you about the attack."

Amanda's mind raced. This wasn't the first time Cassie had returned with signs of abuse. A disturbing pattern was emerging, one that set off alarm bells in Amanda's head. But now wasn't the time to push.

"Alright," Amanda said softly, reaching for antiseptic and bandages. "But I need to treat these wounds. While I do, tell me everything you know about this attack."

"They're like an army of zealots," Cassie said, wincing as Amanda cleaned a particularly deep cut. "And they believe victory is assured. The way they talk about Paradise...it's like they're savoring the idea of punishing the whole community, and especially Samantha."

Amanda felt sick to her stomach. The cult had always been a looming threat, but this...this felt like the beginning of the end. Yet, as she looked at Cassie's battered form, another worry gnawed at her.

"Cassie," she said carefully, helping the woman into a clean shirt. "I have to ask. These injuries... They're becoming a pattern. Is there something you're not telling me? About how you're getting this information?"

Cassie's eyes flashed with a mixture of fear and...was that guilt? "I told you, it's nothing," she insisted. "Just the risks of the mission. Please, Amanda, focus on what matters. Paradise is in danger. You have to warn the others."

Amanda nodded slowly, deciding not to push further for now. Cassie had paid a terrible price for the information she had gathered. The cult must have punished her.

"Okay," Amanda said, helping Cassie to her feet. "I'll alert the others immediately, but Cassie, promise me something."

Cassie looked at her warily. "What?"

"When this is over, when we've dealt with this threat, we're going to talk. Really talk. About everything. Okay?"

For a moment, Cassie looked like she might argue. But then her shoulders slumped, and she gave a small nod. "Okay," she whispered. "If we survive this."

Chapter

The Exodus Plan

Paradise at Night

Deacon was dreaming he was encased in the cocoon again, struggling to stay conscious amid and the growls and snarls that made up the voice.

He was shaken awake. His heart pounded in alarm, but it was Samantha. "Join us in Carl's tent; we're leaving Paradis," she said and rushed away. He was in a daze for a moment but then got dressed as fast as he could. He quickly packed his backpack.

As he hurried to gather his things, a cold pit settled in his stomach. Leaving Paradise felt like abandoning a part of himself. This place, despite all the death and the constant fear, had been his home. The walls, the people, the fights—they had shaped him, hardened him. Now, the thought of leaving behind the community he'd fought so hard for gnawed at him. He shoved his ax and hammer into his belt with a shaky hand, each movement feeling heavier than it should. The rifle was useless without bullets, but he wouldn't leave it behind. It was a part of the fight, like him. His mind raced with questions as he strapped it to his pack: What if they couldn't find another safe place? What if this were the last time he'd see Paradise standing? Doubt flickered, but beneath it, the need to survive overpowered everything else. He had no choice—he had to follow.

He slipped out of his tent, the cold pre-dawn air biting at his face as he moved silently through the sleeping community. The stillness was unnerving, broken only by the distant hoot of an owl. He weaved between the makeshift shelters and the dimly lit paths, careful not to make any noise.

Every shadow felt like a ghost of what he was leaving behind. His hand caressed the top of his ax; it was comforting to feel it by his side. *I can't believe this place is just going to be a memory.* He swallowed hard.

He entered the tent to see Sven, Mary, Cassie, Samantha, Amanda, Billy, the Professor, and Carl gathered in a circle. Leah, Mason, and Joshua were sleeping in the corner. He could immediately see the gravity of their situation weighing heavily on each face—their expressions were a mix of fear, determination, and exhaustion.

Cassie relayed her intelligence about the imminent cult attack, and the room fell into a tense silence. Deacon's mind raced, trying to process the dire reality they faced. The cult was coming with overwhelming force, and behind them, the mega horde that threatened to consume all of California. It was a two-fold threat that seemed impossible to survive.

Are we going to even debate leaving? he wondered. *It looks like there's no point. It's obvious we can't stay.*

The conversation was in hushed tones.

Carl sighed. "If everyone stayed and fought, we don't even have one bullet for each member of the cult," he said, speaking with his eyes closed and his head held in his hands. "We don't have anything to take on the cult's tanks."

Deacon nodded. "Even if we somehow manage to repel the cult, we'd still have to face the horde. And that...that's not a fight we can win." He swallowed hard, the words tasting bitter in his mouth. "I hate to say it, but I agree our only real option is what I suggested to the community. We need to run."

The others nodded slowly, the truth of his words sinking in. But Cassie leaned forward, her face grim. "It's not that simple anymore," she said. "The community...is fracturing. There are three distinct groups forming."

Deacon felt his stomach drop. "What do you mean?" He sat between Samantha and Mary. Mary kissed him on the cheek and rubbed his leg affectionately.

Cassie took a deep breath and continued, "One group has decided to side with the cult. They plan to arrest Deacon and Samantha and hand you both over when the cult arrives." She looked at them apologetically. They think this act might persuade the cult to spare the rest of them."

Samantha's fists clenched, her jaw tight with anger. "Peter's followers," she almost spat the words out. She reached out and rubbed Deacon's shoulder. "What they wanted to do to Deacon was unforgivable."

Deacon remembered how the cult had almost burned Samantha alive the last time they got their hands on her. She had killed their prophet and exposed their conspiracy with the President to manufacture the outbreak. He had never imagined his community would turn against him until Peter had pinned him down, ready to beat him, and the mob looked on gleefully.

I am done with Paradise. I am done with the people here, he thought.

"The second group," Cassie continued, "wants to flee north, like you suggested, Deacon. But..." She hesitated. "They don't want you or Samantha with them. They're afraid having you along will encourage the cult to pursue them."

Deacon felt a pang of hurt at this revelation. After everything they'd been through, after all they'd sacrificed for Paradise, to be cast aside like this...

"And the third group?" Amanda asked, her voice tight with worry.

"That's us," Cassie said. "Me and about thirty others. We want to stick with you and follow your lead. We still believe in you, Deacon, and in all of you."

Deacon shifted uncomfortably. *In me?*

After the battle for Paradise and his role in defeating their attackers, Deacon knew that some people thought of him as a heroic leader, but really, he knew he had just got lucky and that, at one point, he had almost run away into the forest, abandoning everyone to their fate. *If they knew how scared I had been, no one would think of me as a hero.*

The weight of their trust settled on Deacon's shoulders, both a comfort and a burden. He looked at the Professor, an idea forming in his mind. "Can I talk to you for a second?" he asked, gesturing to the corner of the room.

They stepped away from the others; Deacon lowered his voice. "If there's only 30 or, I guess, 40 of us, why don't we go to the bunker? It's secure, well-stocked—"

The Professor nodded.

Then, another thought struck Deacon. "What if we tell them we're going to the Farallon Islands? It's isolated, defensible. We could get them on board with that, then reveal the truth about the bunker once we're underway. That way, no one who is left behind can reveal our true destination to the cult."

The Professor's eyes lit up. "That...that is a good idea."

They rejoined the group. The Professor turned to Cassie. "Gather your thirty people. Tell them we're fleeing to the Farallon Islands. Emphasize the strategic advantages—isolation and defensibility. But make sure they understand the risks too. This won't be an easy journey."

Cassie nodded, determination etched on her face. "I'll make sure they're ready."

Deacon felt a glimmer of hope. In many ways, it was a defeat. They had left the bunker less than a year ago, determined to defeat the cult and the growlers, and now they were heading back with a sorry group of survivors. They had killed hundreds of thousands of growlers and freed several local communities from the cult, but now, all of that was being undone.

The next few hours passed in a blur of furtive activity. Under the cover of darkness, they gathered supplies—food, water, medical kits, weapons—anything they could carry that might help them survive the journey to Santa Rosa Island.

They gathered again near the northwest corner of the community.

He felt a presence beside him and turned to see Samantha. Her face was set in grim determination, but he could see the fear lurking in her eyes. One by one, the rest of the group gathered in the shadows.

Amanda was carrying Joshua. Samantha held Mason and Leah's hands.

Deacon took one last look at Paradise. The community that had been their haven, their hope for a new beginning, now felt like a trap ready to spring shut.

"We're as ready as we'll ever be. It's time," whispered Billy.

Deacon looked back and thought he saw someone observing them from the shadows behind a tent. A flicker of moonlight revealed emptiness. *I must have imagined it.*

Chapter

ESCAPE TO SEA

Encounter in the Woods

The group had gathered in the northwest corner of the community.

Samantha's hands trembled as she zipped up her backpack, the weight of guilt pressing down on her shoulders like a physical force. Every face she saw, every whispered conversation she overheard, felt like an indictment. *All these souls, including Cassie and her followers, all risking everything on this desperate gambit, and it is my fault they have to leave. I am the one who killed the so-called prophet. If I wasn't here the cult would probably have left them alone.*

She had been asked to be in charge of Leah and Mason for the exodus. She held their hands and hoped she would be able to keep them safe. They looked excited to be up in the middle of the night, sneaking around.

I'd love to be a kid right now, she thought. *It would be so nice not to know how much danger we are in. The danger that I have put everyone in. If my presence gets these kids killed ...*

"You okay?" Amanda's voice startled her from her spiral of self-recrimination. She had Joshua on her hip.

Samantha forced a smile that felt more like a grimace. "Fine. Just...making sure we have everything."

Amanda's eyes, filled with a mixture of concern and understanding, searched Samantha's face. "It's not your fault, you know. We're all here because we choose to be."

Before Samantha could respond, Billy approached, his face grim in the moonlight. "Dawn is imminent. We're as ready as we'll ever be. It's time."

Samantha nodded, swallowing hard against the lump in her throat. She looked around Paradise. *You know what? I won't miss this place at all. I almost burned to death in the central square. The people here were content to watch.* She felt a pang of guilt. *We're abandoning those that abandoned us,* she told herself, but she didn't feel absolved from guilt.

She took up a position near the middle of the group as they crept into the night, her eyes constantly scanning for threats. She had a gun on her back, a knife sheathed on one hip, and a tomahawk on her other hip. They had all stopped to share what meager ammunition they had.

If we get into a fight, it better be a short one, she mused.

In order to avoid the main gate, they had set up ladders at the northwest corner of the community. Billy and Sven had volunteered to be on guard at that corner so they would hopefully avoid being seen leaving.

As the group moved through the trees, the air was cool, carrying the strong scent of pine and other vegetation, but every now and then, the sounds of tiny creatures scuttling away from their path broke the silence. Samantha glanced up at the sky, now a pale gray; the sun was creeping over the horizon. Shadows began to lift, stretching into the trees and giving shape to the world around them. She gripped the hands of Leah and Mason a little tighter, hoping that the growing light would bring safety but fearing it would only expose them.

They had barely made it half a mile when Billy, who was on point, suddenly raised his fist—the signal to stop. Samantha's blood ran cold as she heard the unmistakable distant sound of growlers.

"A scattered horde," Deacon whispered. "A small one, maybe just a hundred. They're between us and the boats."

Samantha furrowed her brow.

Billy gestured for everyone to be quiet and listen. "We cannot go back. We must move forward stealthily. Guns are our last resort. If we need to kill, then we must try to do it silently."

Cassie unsheathed both her weapons. "We got this," she whispered. Leah, Mason, you stay by my side." She bent down to make eye contact with them. "I am serious. You stick to me like glue."

They looked up wide-eyed and nodded.

Samantha looked at Carl, with his prosthetic leg, a potential liability in the uneven, wooded terrain. *How can he walk stealthily, let alone fight?*

The tension gripped her stomach as they resumed moving forward. Samantha's every sense was on high alert, her eyes straining in the darkness to distinguish shadow from threat. The first growler they encountered was alone, shambling aimlessly between the trees. It emerged near Cassie but brushed past her, seemingly focused on Carl, but it was Cassie who dealt with it. She moved so quickly and efficiently that it startled Samantha. Her knife crunched into its temple before it had a chance to growl its alert. Then, in the blink of an eye, she thrust her knife into the base of the skull of another growler before Samantha had even spotted it.

Wow! She's incredible. But… it was weird the way it brushed past her like that.

As they pressed on, Samantha found herself constantly checking on Carl. His face was a mask of concentration, every step a potential disaster. The uneven ground and protruding roots made his progress painfully slow. *The apocalypse is no place for someone with a disability.*

A small growler emerged from a thicket near Carl. Samantha's eyes widened. She was sure it would howl or growl before he could dispatch it, but Carl twirled around and buried his knife in its skull in a powerful downward plunge. The growler collapsed. Carl momentarily lost his balance and fell back but immediately got back up and resumed moving forward.

I got to learn to be less judgmental, Samantha though. *He was an FBI agent before the outbreak. They make them tough.*

They were forced to dispatch several more growlers along the way. Each encounter was a heart-stopping ordeal. Samantha watched as Billy expertly took down one with his hunting knife, the creature's body falling with a soft thud that seemed to echo in the night. Then, he quietly eliminated another.

When I met Billy, he was an overweight computer nerd; now he's kicking ass and leading us out of here.

They neared a small clearing, and Samantha's blood ran cold. A cluster of at least a dozen growlers stood between them and the path to the boats. Billy signaled the group to fall back. They would have to find another way.

One of the growlers must have seen Billy because its head snapped to face him. It threw its head back, and Samantha knew what would happen next. It would let loose that all-too-familiar growl and howl to alert the whole horde, but instead, the hilt of a knife appeared between its eyes.

Cassie had thrown it. She lunged forward, carrying an ax in each hand. Her movements were a blur. It almost seemed like the growlers were stunned by her artistry. They watched but did not attack. She whirled and sliced and hacked her way through the group. None of the growlers made a noise, and in less than thirty seconds, she had cleared them all.

Jesus! I never would have believed it if I hadn't seen it, thought Samantha. *She's like someone from an action movie where each move has been planned and choreographed for months. What IS her story? It was like even the growlers were frozen in shock watching her kill.*

Just as she was marveling at Cassie, the sound of a gunshot filled the night air. It came from Paradise.

The sound of growls erupted from all directions.

A search beam from Paradise scanned the woods.

"Run!" shouted Billy, all pretense of stealth abandoned. "To the boats, now!"

As chaos erupted around her, Samantha found herself torn between the desperate need to reach safety and the urge to protect Leah and Mason. She saw Deacon helping Carl who had tripped, the agent's face twisted in pain and frustration.

Cassie was now spearheading the group's progress, hacking her way through any growler that blocked their path.

Paradise speakers crackled to life. "Catch the fucking traitors." Armed men ran out of the gates only to find growlers in the ditches. Gunfire intensified.

Samantha watched as Deacon raised his gun, picking off the closest threats with practiced precision, but for every growler that fell, two more seemed to take its place. The night air filled with the sounds of combat—the thud of melee weapons, the sharp cracks of gunfire, the snarls of the growlers.

As they neared the edge of the clearing, Samantha's heart soared. She could see the river through the trees, the outline of their boats just visible in the dawn light. They were going to make it.

"Keep moving!" she shouted, her voice hoarse. "We're almost there!"

As they broke through the tree line onto the riverbank, Samantha allowed herself a moment of hope. The boats were there, hidden under branches just as Billy had promised. They were within reach of escape.

But as she turned to usher the last of their group toward safety, Samantha's blood ran cold. The commotion had not gone unnoticed by the rest of Paradise. She could see figures emerging from the settlement, running toward them with weapons raised.

Among them, she recognized Peter, his face contorted with rage and triumph. "They're here!" his voice carried over the chaos. "The traitors are escaping! Don't let them get away!"

She realized with a jolt that this was the group that had allied with the cult, the ones who had promised to hand over her and Deacon. The desperation in their voices was clear—they knew that if she and Deacon escaped, their deal with the cult would be meaningless. The cult would be unforgiving.

"Billy!" Samantha shouted over the din of battle. "Get those boats ready! We need to move!"

Billy nodded grimly, sprinting toward the concealed vessels. Samantha turned her attention back to the approaching threat, her mind racing to formulate a plan. They were caught between the growlers and their former neighbors, neither of which would show mercy.

Cassie organized several men into a rear guard action, spraying bullets at Peter's men. "Get in the boats; we'll cover you," she shouted.

Samantha dragged Mason and Leah through the bushes toward the boats. The children were doing their best not to slow her down.

"We don't need to take them alive!" shouted Peter. "We can just show the Phoenix their bodies."

Bullets zipped through the air, making Samantha duck as she ran.

Ahead of her, Billy, Carl, the Professor, and Deacon were slashing through wandering growlers. She realized, with horror, that they must have all run out of ammunition. They released the moorings on the boats and Amanda and Samantha boarded with the children.

Cassie and the thirty other volunteers joined them, maintaining covering fire.

Each sailboat had small engines, which very slowly eased them out into the river. The rate of gunfire slowly reduced.

They must realize they won't be able to get my body now. They'll have to flee north with the rest of the community. And so ends Paradise.

As the boats cut through the choppy waters, Samantha felt a momentary sense of relief wash over her. She turned to look back, watching Paradise, their home for so long, fade into the distance.

The weight of their narrow escape still pressed on her chest, but for now, they were safe.

Billy's voice broke through her reverie, his tone grim. "I've done an ammo count," he announced. "Most of us used everything we had during the escape. We've got maybe fifty rounds total, spread across a few half-empty magazines."

The news sent a ripple of unease through the group. Fifty rounds wouldn't get them far if they encountered any significant threats. Samantha saw fear creeping back into the eyes of their companions.

Deacon cleared his throat, drawing everyone's attention. "There's something you all need to know," he said, his young face set with determination. "We're not heading to the Farallon Islands. Our real destination is Santa Rosa Island. There's a secure bunker there, one the cult believes is permanently sealed, but we know a secret entrance."

Samantha observed the mixed reactions rippling through their small band of survivors. Some faces lit up with hope at the prospect of a safe haven, while others darkened with suspicion at the revelation of this deception.

Before the situation could escalate, Samantha stepped in to explain the bunker's resources, drawing on the knowledge she'd gained during her time undercover with the cult. As she spoke, she saw the tension in the group begin to ease, replaced by cautious optimism. "There's enough food to last us for years. There are all the modern conveniences: clean running water, hot showers, climate control, a fully stocked hospital, and a very well-stocked armory. We will be safe there."

"Are there growlers there?" someone asked.

Samantha smiled. "No... well, yes, there are, but they are all locked up in a room they cannot escape."

In the midst of this, Samantha's gaze fell on Cassie. For the first time since they'd met, the woman looked truly relaxed, almost content. The constant wariness that had shadowed her features seemed to have lifted.

However, Samantha's relief at seeing Cassie's improved state was short-lived. She noticed how the other community members seemed to be deliberately avoiding looking at Cassie, creating a bubble of isolation around her even in the cramped confines of the boat.

Anger flared in Samantha's chest. After everything Cassie had done for them, she was still being treated as an outsider. When would she find the friendship and support she so clearly deserved?

Samantha found herself drawn into memories of her own time undercover in the cult. The constant fear of discovery, the crushing loneliness, the strain of maintaining a false persona day after day—it all came flooding back. She remembered the nights she'd lain awake, questioning every interaction, every word spoken, wondering if today would be the day her cover was blown.

Looking at Cassie now, Samantha recognized the same shadows in her eyes, the same careful control of her expressions and movements. The similarities in their experiences struck her forcefully, igniting a deep sense of empathy.

Without hesitation, Samantha made her way across the boat to where Cassie sat. She lowered herself down beside the woman and, in a gesture that felt both natural and necessary, put a comforting arm around her shoulders.

Cassie stiffened for a moment before gradually relaxing into the embrace.

"You know," Samantha began softly, "I understand more than most what you've been through. The isolation, the constant fear, the weight of carrying secrets that could get you killed if discovered."

As Samantha spoke, sharing some of her own experiences and the toll they had taken, she felt Cassie gradually relax further. The woman's breathing steadied, and some of the ever-present tension seemed to drain from her body.

"I just want you to know," Samantha concluded, "that you're not alone anymore. What you've done, the risks you've taken for us—they matter. You matter. And I've got your back, always."

Cassie turned to look at Samantha, and in her eyes, Samantha saw a complex mix of emotions. Gratitude was there, certainly, shining bright and genuine. But there was something else, too, something Samantha couldn't quite identify. It was gone in a flash, replaced by a small, hesitant smile.

Samantha observed Cassie's reactions carefully, and she couldn't shake the feeling that something wasn't quite right.

This woman has been through so much, yet she just doesn't carry herself like victims I've seen. She doesn't have the anger that I carry. Am I weaker than her? I treat men like a threat. Yet she walks amongst the men here as if they should be frightened of her. God I wish I had her confidence.

Samantha watched as Cassie's gaze scanned the room and settled on a large man, whose name Samantha did not know. Cassie licked her lips.

Whoa! She's been assaulted by men, yet she is drawn to the most muscular ones.

The man noticed Cassie staring and a look of fear flashed over his face.

What was that? Some non-verbal communication happened just there. Why would he show fear of her? Why doesn't she show fear of him? What is going on?

The sun climbed higher in the sky. Samantha took a deep breath, her arm still around Cassie. For now, they were safe. For now, they had hope. For now, that would have to be enough, but she understood that Cassie held secrets. She had a relationship with some of the people who had chosen to join them, and the dynamics of that relationship did not make sense.

Why would people fear Cassie?

Chapter

The Bunker

The entrance to the long passageway

The gentle rocking of the boat had become a constant companion. Deacon leaned against the railing, his eyes scanning the horizon for any sign of Santa Rosa Island. The morning mist and salty breeze ruffled his hair, carrying with it the promise of a new beginning.

Mary sidled up next to him, her shoulder brushing against his. "Penny for your thoughts?" she asked, a small smile playing on her lips. Her hand pulled him at his waist to bring their bodies together.

Deacon turned to her, feeling a warmth spread through his chest despite the cool ocean air. "Just thinking about what's waiting for us," he said. "It's hard to believe we might finally have a safe place, you know?"

Mary nodded, her eyes reflecting the same mix of hope and apprehension that Deacon felt. "I know. After everything we've been through, it almost seems too good to be true. I really wonder why you guys ever left it."

"We thought we could do some good on the mainland. We brought them the vaccine." *It all seems somewhat naïve now. Maybe we just made things worse. Maybe life under a religious dictatorship would be better for them.* He looked at Mary and remembered what kind of life she would have had with the perverted clergy. *I have to keep reminding myself the cult are not remotely Christian. They have no morality. They don't even pretend to be moral.*

They stood in comfortable silence for a moment, the rhythmic sound of waves lapping against the boat filling the air. Deacon found his gaze drawn to Cassie, sitting alone near the stern. The people that had joined them seemed to be avoiding her. The woman who had endured so much, yet had the strength to help them all escape. His heart swelled with admiration and sympathy.

"I'm glad Cassie's with us," Deacon said softly. "After everything she's been through with the cult, she deserves some peace. She deserves to be loved by us all, to know what true friends can feel like."

Mary squeezed his hand. "You have a good heart, Deacon. I'm sure having friends like us will help her heal."

A movement caught Deacon's eye, pulling his attention away from Cassie. Amanda and the Professor were huddled together near the cabin, their heads close as they whispered intently. Curious, Deacon watched them, noting the tension in their postures.

Suddenly, Amanda's eyes flicked towards Cassie, her brow furrowing slightly. The Professor followed her gaze, his expression unreadable. They exchanged a look that Deacon couldn't decipher before resuming their hushed conversation.

Deacon frowned, a small knot of confusion forming in his stomach. Why were they looking at Cassie like that? And why all the secrecy?

He watched as Amanda made her way across the deck, ostensibly to check on various members of their group. But Deacon noticed how her path seemed to deliberately avoid Cassie, and how her eyes would dart towards the woman when she thought no one was looking.

The Professor, meanwhile, had struck up a conversation with Billy. From where Deacon stood, it looked like a casual chat, but he couldn't help noticing how the Professor kept Cassie in his peripheral vision, his body angled to keep her in sight.

"Hey," Mary's voice broke through his observations. "You okay? You went quiet there for a minute."

Deacon shook his head, trying to dispel the odd feeling that had come over him. "Yeah, sorry. Just got lost in thought, I guess."

He glanced back at Amanda and the Professor, then at Cassie. It didn't make sense. Amanda was always so caring, and the Professor had welcomed Cassie with open arms when she first arrived at Paradise. Why did they seem so... wary of her now?

Maybe I'm reading too much into things, Deacon thought. *We're all tired and stressed. I'm probably just imagining it.*

Still, as he turned back to Mary, forcing a smile and changing the subject to their hopes for the bunker, Deacon couldn't quite shake the feeling that something was off. The image of Amanda and the Professor's furtive glances stayed with him, a small splinter of unease in his otherwise hopeful outlook.

It's nothing, he told himself firmly. *We're almost at the island. Soon, we'll all be safe, and everything will be fine.*

But even as he thought it, Deacon found his eyes drawn back to the strange dance playing out on the deck, his mind struggling to make sense of what he was seeing.

"Look!" Mary pointed.

Deacon's heart drummed as Santa Rosa Island loomed from the fog, its jagged outline taking shape against the pale light of dawn. The island felt less like salvation and more like an apparition—its cliffs rising like ancient, weathered sentinels from the sea, shrouded in mist that clung to the shore like a veil hiding secrets. He knew there were secrets on that island. He had almost died there. He had been cocooned there.

Deacon felt a subtle tremor in his limbs that spread like a slow burn beneath his skin. His fingers twitched, restless, as if searching for something to hold onto, while his muscles tensed and released in rapid succession, an invisible force pulling them tight. His chest felt constricted, not painfully, but enough to make every breath feel slightly off, as though the air around him was growing too thick. He took a deep breath in and slowly released it.

He squinted into the gray haze, trying to discern details, but the island remained stubbornly distant, its rocky silhouette giving nothing away. He had wanted the island to feel like a refuge, a break from the constant fear that had stalked them since Paradise. Yet, as the island emerged from the mist, he realized how little they really knew about it. They knew the bunker existed, but what other secrets might there be? Maybe the cult had performed terrible experiments on the island. Maybe thousands of growlers had washed ashore and were waiting to surprise them. Maybe the growlers they had trapped in the bunker had broken free.

Deacon's fingers tightened on the boat's edge, his knuckles white. This place felt too remote, too untouched by human hands, as if it had been waiting for them, not to offer shelter, but to swallow them whole.

Their small flotilla approached the wooden dock.

Once docked, Billy tapped him on the shoulder. "How about you show everyone the way to the entrance?"

"Me?" said Deacon with uncertainty.

Billy looked questioningly. "You remember the way, right?"

Deacon nodded. "Um, sure. Alright, everyone," Deacon called out, his voice carrying over the lapping waves. "Okay."

He led the way up a rocky path, the crunch of gravel underfoot barely masking the rustle of wind through the dense underbrush. Every step seemed to drag him deeper into the island's eerie silence, the usual sounds of life—birds, insects—eerily absent. His breath came shallow and quick, the humid air clinging to his skin. The others followed close behind, their presence both a comfort and a weight pressing down on him. The twisting trail forced them to weave through low-hanging branches and jagged rocks, the dark shapes shifting in the corner of his vision.

He froze. Up ahead, a hulking figure lurked between two trees, motionless. His pulse spiked, fingers tightening around his ac. He took a few more steps toward it, and the shape resolved into nothing more than a twisted, gnarled tree, its shadow playing tricks on his mind. *Sheeze!* He exhaled shakily, trying to steady himself.

"Don't go jumping at shadows," whispered Mary. "Or you'll freak everyone out."

The tension in his muscles didn't ease, and with every step, he imagined the island to grow more alive, more aware of their presence.

There was commotion behind him. Deacon turned to see that Carl had fallen. *Oh shit, I should be moving slower for him.*

"Let's take a five-minute break," shouted Billy.

Deacon nodded and took out two strips of dried rabbit meat. He gave one to Mary and started chewing on the other. After a couple of minutes, his gaze fell on the Professor and Amanda. They were engaged in an intense, whispered conversation, their faces etched with concern. Curiosity piqued, Deacon tried to edge closer, straining to catch snippets of their discussion.

"...not sure how long we can..." Amanda's voice drifted to him.

"...have to be certain before we..." the Professor replied, his tone urgent.

Before Deacon could hear more, Billy called out to him. "Hey, kid! I think we can resume. We are all anxious to get there."

Deacon moved away from the hushed conversation, focusing instead on the task of leading them to the entrance.

He slowed his pace for Carl, but ten minutes later, they arrived at the entrance. He pushed aside a growth of tree limbs to reveal the outer entrance; then he realized something. "We need a flashlight. I don't have …"

Billy ran up and placed a flashlight in his hands.

"Thank you," said Deacon, gripping the flashlight as he turned toward the passageway. His palms were slick with sweat, and he wiped them on his pants before leading the group into the narrow, downward-sloping corridor. Every step echoed in the confined space, the dull thud of boots on stone amplifying his sense of unease.

He wished the flashlight was brighter so he could see further down the passageway. What if there were growlers down there? Being at the front, he would have to deal with them, and he'd have to fight while holding the flashlight. He reminded himself it was unlikely that there would be any growlers, but his imagination was hard to quell.

His mind raced as they descended, imagining what might be waiting behind the doors below. He had been here before, but the island had a way of twisting even familiar places into something ominous. His thoughts kept circling back to the growlers—locked up the last time they were here. But what if something had gone wrong? What if somehow they had opened the door from the cocooning chamber?

The dim beam of his flashlight flickered over the walls, revealing the same slick concrete and rusted fixtures. Yet every shadow seemed to crawl, every whisper of air like a breath on his neck. His pulse quickened with each corner they rounded, making his chest tighten further. He heard a growl, and his heart seemed to stop, then he realized it was coming from his stomach. He could feel the others behind him, their footsteps close. They must have seen him startled and wondered what was going on.

Why did Billy have me lead while he hangs back with the Professor and Amanda? Something isn't right with them.

They reached the door at the end of the passage, and Deacon's breath hitched. He knew what lay beyond—the strangest room in the bunker. He had always hated it, with its unsettling hooks and loops on the wall forming a giant X, as if waiting for some twisted ritual to take place. The weird table in the center had attachments he didn't understand, contraptions that resembled medieval torture devices. He had asked about it once, and the adults had shut him down quickly, their refusal to explain only adding to the room's sinister aura. Now, standing before the door, the fear that something had changed gnawed at him.

His hand trembled slightly as he reached for the handle, hesitating for a moment. He glanced back at the group, their faces dimly lit by his beam, a mix of worry and anticipation. There was no turning back now. He twisted the knob, pushing the door open with a loud creak that seemed to reverberate through the entire bunker.

The room was just as he remembered. The X on the wall. The bizarre tools hanging in neat rows. No growlers. *Thank God!* He exhaled, relief flooding him for a brief second, but it was short-lived. He crossed the room quickly, refusing to linger, leading them through the next door into the rest of the bunker. This was the late prophet's secret escape route, the path that would take them to safety—at least for now.

As they moved through the main areas—the living quarters, the mess hall, the medical bay, the command center—Deacon saw the awe in the faces of his companions. Relief mingled with surprise as they took in the advanced technology surrounding them, a contrast to the harsh, primitive conditions they'd endured in Paradise. But Deacon couldn't shake the feeling that something was still wrong. Every door they passed felt like it was hiding something. Every quiet hum of machinery reminded him that the growlers were still here, somewhere, locked behind walls. Or were they?

By the time they reached the long corridor leading to the cocooning chamber, the tension had wound so tight in Deacon's chest he could barely breathe. "There's something you all need to know," he said, gesturing to the wall of the corridor. This is a concealed door and behind are thousands of trapped growlers. "Actually, we don't know how many are back there. We killed a lot of them, but there are still many inside."

Maybe one day, we will deal with the remainder.

Deacon pointed at a small hole in the wall, the lock. "The door can only be opened with a special key or through the central computer, so we should be safe,"

At this revelation, a ripple of unease passed through the group. Deacon saw fear flicker in some eyes while others nodded in grim understanding.

As the initial tour concluded, Deacon observed the varied reactions to their new home. Some seemed to relax, the bunker's security allowing them to let down their guard. Others appeared overwhelmed, almost claustrophobic in the enclosed space.

Later, as the group dispersed to explore their new surroundings, Deacon found himself drawn to the medical bay. Through the open door, he spotted Amanda meticulously cataloging supplies in the pharmacy. Her focus was intense, her movements precise as she inventoried their medical resources.

She must be so relieved to finally have modern medical equipment and supplies.

Watching her work, Deacon felt a surge of admiration. Amanda's skills had saved countless lives in Paradise, often working with the barest minimum of supplies. Here, with a fully stocked pharmacy at her disposal, her potential to help seemed limitless.

For a moment, Deacon considered approaching her, asking about the conversation he'd overheard earlier with the Professor, but something held him back. The serious expressions, the hushed tones—whatever they were discussing, it was clear they weren't ready to share it yet. Reluctantly, he decided to respect their privacy, at least for now.

Instead, he made his way to the communications center. The array of radio equipment was impressive, far more advanced than anything they'd had access to in Paradise. With careful adjustments, they might be able to reach other survivor groups and perhaps even establish a network of allies.

Deacon's mind wandered to the threats they'd left behind. The cult would surely be furious at their escape. *The mega-horde...how long before it reaches Paradise?* Had they doomed their former home by leaving?

The bunker offered safety, yes, but it also felt like a gilded cage. They were secure for now, but for how long? The cult knew about the bunker, though they probably didn't know about the secret entrance.

The bunker was a sanctuary, a place to regroup and plan. But it couldn't be their final destination. Sooner or later, they would have to venture out again and face the dangers of the world they'd left behind.

Chapter

Feast of Fools

Cassie and Her Followers Make their Move

For their first night in the bunker, Billy had suggested a feast using the bunker's plentiful supplies.

Deacon felt his muscles aching as he helped Billy hang the last of the makeshift decorations in the bunker's main hall. The space, usually stark and utilitarian, had been transformed into something almost festive. Strings of Christmas lights cast a warm glow over the gathered survivors, and the air was thick with the aroma of cooking food—real food, not the meager rations they'd subsisted on for months.

"Not bad, kid," Billy said, clapping Deacon on the shoulder. "Almost looks like a real party in here."

Deacon nodded, allowing himself a small smile. It did look good, and more importantly, it felt good. For the first time since they'd fled Paradise, people were relaxing, letting their guard down.

The constant tension that had become a part of daily life seemed to be melting away, replaced by an atmosphere of cautious optimism.

He noticed Amanda was spending a lot of time in the infirmary and she had locked the door. *She's probably getting reacquainted with the supplies and equipment there and doesn't want to be disturbed.*

He busied himself setting the table and noticed even Cassie had become more active, interacting with some of the exiles from Paradise. She even seemed to be quietly giving them orders. He noticed how she would go to each person and whisper to them, then they would rush away to carry out her requests.

Finally, she is coming out of her shell. Gaining the confidence to talk to people, even if it is all in whispers. One day she will be confident enough to speak out loud.

His heart warmed to see her. He gave her a big smile, which she noticed. Her expression flashed from confusion to polite smile to … something else which Deacon couldn't quite discern.

She seems to be more comfortable with the strangers, the people I didn't know from Paradise. It's almost as if they knew her.

They had all been warned about the growlers locked in the cocooning chamber. After that everyone had insisted on being armed, so Billy had opened up the armory and handed out weapons. It was going to be a rule in the bunker, that all the adults be armed at all times. That way if there were any surprises, they'd be able to respond.

We really need to take care of those growlers. Even if they are locked up, I won't be able to sleep properly while they're still active.

It was the Professor, of all people, who had announced a feast to celebrate their safe arrival at the bunker. Everyone had responded with great enthusiasm. Their first bunker meal was going to be a good one.

Throughout the preparations, the Professor seemed distracted, furtive even. Deacon figured that the Professor was not used to frivolous things like feasts. He was a man of science, more comfortable in a lab than in a social setting.

Deacon found himself swept up in the jovial mood once the feast was underway. Laughter echoed off the bunker walls, punctuated by the clink of glasses and the scrape of utensils on plates. It was almost possible to forget, for a moment, the dangers that lurked outside their sanctuary.

That is until Deacon tried to pour himself a glass of the wine Amanda had retrieved from the prophet's private cellar.

"Whoa there, young man," Amanda said, swooping in to intercept the bottle. "I don't think so. You're still underage."

Deacon felt a flash of frustration. "Seriously? After everything we've been through, everything I've done, I'm still too young for a drink?"

Amanda's expression softened, but she stood firm. "Rules are rules, Deacon. We need to maintain some sense of normalcy, especially now."

Deacon wanted to argue further, to point out the absurdity of clinging to pre-apocalypse drinking laws in their current situation. But he bit his tongue, not wanting to disrupt the celebratory mood.

Instead, he grabbed a cup of water and tried to push down his annoyance.

As the evening wore on, Deacon found himself starting to enjoy the festivities despite his earlier frustration. At one point he noticed that some of the escapees from Paradise were clustering together. *I guess it's only natural to form cliques,* he thought. Some of them moved closer to the exits, their postures tense and alert. *I wonder if they're going to have their own party afterwards. I hope they invite me.*

He was in the middle of a conversation with Carl about potential improvements to the bunker's security systems when a hush fell over the room. A glass shattered somewhere, making everyone jump.

Cassie had stood and raised a gun she had kept under her jacket, and she wasn't alone. All thirty of her volunteers who had joined their escape from Paradise were also suddenly holding guns. Gone was the grateful, somewhat timid demeanor they had displayed earlier. Now, they stood tall and confident, most of them grimly smiling or sneering.

Cassie's voice, when she spoke, was filled with an authority Deacon had never heard from her before. "I want to thank you all for your hospitality," she said, her words dripping with false sweetness. "But I'm afraid there's been a change of plans."

"You see," Cassie continued, her followers fanning out around the room, effectively surrounding the unsuspecting feast-goers, "this bunker doesn't belong to you anymore. It's mine now. We're taking over."

After her statement, there was a long silence. Deacon's mind raced, trying to process this sudden betrayal. He realized with a sinking feeling that their brief moment of peace had been nothing but an illusion. The woman he had thought was their ally, their savior even, was transforming before his eyes into something monstrous.

"You're probably wondering what's going on," Cassie said, her voice smug. "Allow me to enlighten you. You see, I am the genius behind the virus. The mastermind of this brave new world."

She actually calls herself a genius; who does that? thought Deacon.

He felt his stomach lurch at the pride in her voice as she claimed responsibility for the devastation that had claimed millions of lives. His skin felt like ice was trickling down his body.

"I planned it all," Cassie continued, clearly relishing her moment in the spotlight. "The virus, the Black—I coded them myself. Quite the accomplishment, don't you think?"

She began to pace the room, her armed followers maintaining their positions around the stunned group.

Cassie's words slammed into Deacon like a physical force. His chest constricted, each breath becoming a deliberate, painful effort. The edges of his vision darkened, the faces around him blurring into indistinct shapes. A high-pitched ringing filled his ears, drowning out the sudden commotion in the room.

His mind reeled, grasping for some semblance of sense in this new, twisted reality. Memories flashed before him: Cassie's kind smile as she comforted a child in Paradise, her fierce determination as she fought alongside them. Each recollection now tainted, corrupted by the venom of her true nature.

Deacon's fingers tingled, a prickling sensation that spread up his arms and across his scalp. He pressed his palms against the rough fabric of his pants, desperate for any sensation to ground him in reality. The coarse texture beneath his fingertips stood in stark contrast to the unreality of the moment.

A wave of nausea rolled through him, bitter bile rising in his throat. He swallowed hard, the acrid taste lingering on his tongue, a physical manifestation of the disgust and betrayal roiling within him.

His mind raced, a frantic loop of disbelief and dawning horror. How many deaths lay at her feet? How many lives destroyed for her twisted game? And they had welcomed her, protected her, mourned with her. The weight of their collective naivety pressed down on him, threatening to crush him beneath its enormity.

How could I be so absolutely oblivious. She fooled me so completely I … I am so stupid.

His gaze locked onto Cassie's face, searching for any hint of the person he thought he knew. But her features, once familiar and trusted, now seemed alien and malevolent. The curve of her smile, the glint in her eyes – how had he never seen the cruelty lurking just beneath the surface?

As the full implications of Cassie's words sank in, Deacon felt something shift inside him. A hardness formed in the pit of his stomach, a cold, dense knot of anger and resolve. The world as he knew it had shattered, but from the fragments, a new understanding began to take shape.

He clenched his jaw, teeth grinding as he fought to regain control of his faculties. This was no time for shock or self-pity. They were in danger, all of them, and he needed to be ready. With effort, he forced his attention outward, assessing the room, cataloging potential threats and allies.

The betrayal cut deep, a wound that would leave a scar. But as Deacon met the eyes of his companions, seeing his own shock and determination mirrored back at him, he knew this wasn't the end. It was a beginning – the start of a fight they couldn't afford to lose.

"I thought it was the cult," said Deacon, his voice hoarse, cracking with emotion.

"The cult? They were just pawns. Useful idiots to build up supplies for my chosen survivors and to initiate the spread of the virus. Oh, and that army of 7,500 soldiers and tanks? A complete fabrication. I can't believe you fell for that."

Deacon's mind was spinning, trying to process the enormity of what he was hearing. He glanced at the Professor, expecting to see shock or outrage, but the older man's face was a mask of calm. It was unsettling.

Cassie paced the room, her movements predatory, eyes gleaming with a mix of pride and barely contained rage. She began to explain her grand plan, her voice dripping with self-satisfaction.

"I coded the identities of my 'chosen ones' into the growlers themselves," she said, pausing for effect. "I call it 'imprinting.' It ensures they'll never be attacked."

Deacon's mind reeled. He thought of all the times they'd narrowly escaped growler attacks, of the friends they'd lost. All of it orchestrated by the woman standing before them. His fists clenched at his sides, knuckles white with suppressed fury.

Cassie continued, oblivious to or perhaps reveling in the horror on their faces. "The imperfect vaccine I gave to the cult? That was by design. I knew it would fail after a year."

The Professor's eyebrows shot up at this, a flicker of grudging admiration crossing his face before being replaced by disgust. Deacon glanced at him, confused by the reaction. Did the Professor understand something about the science that Deacon was missing?

"Everything was going according to plan," Cassie said, her voice taking on an edge of irritation. She turned abruptly, fixing the Professor with a glare. "Until you had to go and create a real vaccine."

The Professor met her gaze steadily, his calm demeanor a stark contrast to Cassie's growing agitation. Deacon marveled at his composure. How could he be so collected in the face of this madness?

Cassie's voice rose, filled with indignation. "I couldn't have that, could I? The earth could potentially be contaminated with the unchosen."

She spun again, this time facing Deacon. He flinched involuntarily as her finger jabbed in his direction. "And you," she spat, "somehow you learned to do something only I am supposed to do. Communicating with the hive mind of the horde."

Deacon's breath caught in his throat. The voice he'd heard, the connection he'd felt to the horde – it had all been real. But how? How had he tapped into something Cassie claimed as her exclusive domain?

Cassie's face twisted into a sneer. "So, I sent Nathanial and his little army after you. That failed spectacularly." She laughed bitterly. "Never send a man to do a woman's job. Well... here I am."

A heavy silence fell over the room as the weight of her words sank in. Deacon looked around, seeing shock, disbelief, and dawning horror on the faces of his friends. Mary caught his eye, her expression a mix of fear and determination. She gave him a small nod, as if to say, "We'll get through this."

Amanda broke the silence, her voice shaking with a mixture of anger and disbelief. "But... the abuse? The marks on your back?"

Cassie's laughter cut through the tension, a sound devoid of warmth that sent chills down Deacon's spine. "Oh, honey," she said, her tone mockingly sweet. "Those weren't from abuse. Let's just say I like my sex life a little... rough."

Deacon felt his face flush, a mix of embarrassment and revulsion washing over him. He remembered the sympathy he'd felt for Cassie, the protective instinct her supposed abuse had triggered in him. It had all been a lie.

"Beatings?" Amanda's voice was a mix of horror and disgust. "I thought you were..."

"A victim?" Cassie finished, her eyes glinting with amusement. "Not I. The pain and pleasure centers of the brain are very close to each other; mine overlap." She cocked her head, a challenging smirk on her face. "Don't judge me."

Deacon was mystified. He looked at Billy, seeing his own confusion mirrored in the older man's face. How could someone derive pleasure from such violence? And more importantly, how had they all been so thoroughly deceived?

Cassie locked eyes with Amanda. "Nature makes some people naturally dominant. That's me. I walk into a room and everyone is my bitch. Like now. Look at you all

Some people enjoy pain? I have heard of that think. Then he thought about the fur lined handcuffs.

As Cassie's revelations continued to unfold, Deacon felt as though the ground beneath his feet was crumbling away. Everything he thought he knew, every assumption he'd made about their situation, was being systematically destroyed. And judging by the faces around him, he wasn't alone in feeling utterly lost in this new, twisted reality.

The Professor cleared his throat, his voice steady despite the circumstances. "There's just a couple of things I don't understand. Why did the horde's voice change? How did the horde at Paradise get orders from the horde in Alameda? I never figured that out."

Cassie's eyes lit up at the question. "They didn't. I simply captured a growler and attached a transmitter with speakers and solar panels. With a bit of audio tech, I became the voice for that horde. Simple, really. Once you rescued me, and I was safely embedded in Paradise, I told the horde to join their brethren in Alameda."

She paused, her expression turning almost dreamy. "The mega horde is my final weapon. Soon, it will reach critical mass and sweep aside what's left of humanity. Only my chosen ones will remain."

Deacon couldn't hold back any longer. "But why?" he burst out. "Why do all this? It's all so pointless."

Cassie's laughter cut through the room like a knife. "Oh, you naive boy. I did it because it sounded like fun. I did it just to prove to myself that I could."

The casual admission of genocide for entertainment made Deacon's blood run cold. He felt sick, overwhelmed by the magnitude of Cassie's evil.

"As for why you're still alive," Cassie continued, gesturing to the Professor and Deacon, "you both might prove useful. The rest of you... Well, I'll decide what to do with you in due course."

Deacon glanced again at the Professor, surprised to see the man's calm demeanor unchanged in the face of these earth-shattering revelations. There was something in the older man's eyes, a glint of...was that understanding? It was as if he had expected this, or at least something like it.

Deacon felt a chill run down his spine. What else didn't he know? What other secrets were lurking in the shadows of their supposed sanctuary?

"One final question," said Amanda. "When we met, you sprayed perfume at me. There had to be a reason for that. What was it?"

"My little trick. It rarely works. I tried it on each and every one of you, and no joy. It has a retrovirus in it that imprints my identity as one for you to follow, love, and obey. I cut and paste most of it from ducks. My father banished me from his lab when I tried it on him. Oh well, family drama."

The Professor's calm voice cut through the tension-filled room. "You know, Cassie, often genius is just being in the right place at the right time. I don't think you're as smart as you believe. You were simply interested in DNA when AI-based programming became powerful enough to implement your...peculiar machinations."

Cassie's smug expression faltered for a moment, but she quickly recovered. "You're just jealous of my superior intellect."

The Professor ignored her jab, continuing in the same measured tone. "One of the unique aspects of this bunker is that it has direct communications with the President. Samantha learned that when they interrogated her."

At this, Cassie's composure cracked. Her eyes widened in surprise, a flicker of uncertainty crossing her face.

The Professor turned to a console nearby and pressed a button. "Hello, Mr. President," he said calmly.

"Hello, Professor," came a gravelly voice from the speakers. "I've heard everything."

Cassie's face drained of color as the President continued, "I've just authorized a nuclear strike on the Alameda Naval Base. Cassie, my dear, your mega horde is no more."

"You've made a great mistake," Cassie said, her voice shaking with rage. She turned to her guards. "Kill them all!"

But as she looked around, she found her followers slumped in their seats or on the floor, fast asleep. Samantha stood behind her, a gun trained steadily on Cassie's head.

"Your gun has blanks in it, Cassie," Samantha said coolly, reaching out to take the weapon from Cassie's suddenly limp fingers.

Cassie stood, mouth agape, shock evident on her face. The Professor stepped forward, his calm demeanor never wavering.

The Professor shook his head. "You see, Cassie, we figured you out. It took a lot longer than it should have, but we finally figured you out."

Cassie slumped down into a chair. "How?"

The Professor looked almost sorry for her. "We only realized once you were on board the boat on our way here. You see, the thing about crazy leaders is that their followers look at them...differently. Nervously or with adoration. We noticed how your 30 volunteers looked at you. It wasn't right. Amanda pointed it out to me."

Amanda smiled. “Then we started thinking and looking back at our whole history with you. We suspected you brought the horde that killed Bert. You didn't need rescuing; you were controlling them. Then I thought about when we were leaving Paradise, and I saw you fighting your way through the growlers on the way to the boats… It was as if the growlers were blind to you. None of them grabbed you. None of them saw you as food. I should have realized at the time they just weren’t attacking you."

Deacon watched in awe as the pieces fell into place.

Amanda continued, her voice tight with controlled anger, "One puzzle Billy raised was the radio transmission you supposedly sent from the cult community. The strength of the signal meant it was only a couple of miles away, not where the cult was supposed to be."

“I dismissed it at the time. I thought I was just misunderstanding the technology,” said Billy.

“My puppets?” said Cassie, pointing to her unconscious followers.

Amanda flicked her finger against a wine glass. “My medical expertise was used to concoct something to drug your friends with.”

"And, of course," Billy added, "we made sure that the guns in the armory were loaded with blanks. Just in case."

The Professor rubbed his hands together. “I really wondered how we were going to extract all the information from you. We have ethical concerns about torture. I should have known a megalomaniac like you would have to boast of all their plans. You monologued like a bond villain."

As Amanda moved to secure Cassie and her unconscious followers, Deacon's mind reeled. They had known. Somehow, they had pieced it all together and set this elaborate trap.

The Professor approached Cassie, who was now securely restrained. "The only question I have now, Cassie, is what am I going to do with you all?"

Deacon looked around the room, taking in the unconscious bodies of Cassie's followers, the shocked faces of his friends, and the grim satisfaction on the faces of the Professor and Samantha. The weight of what they had uncovered, the enormity of Cassie's crimes, and the sudden, dramatic reversal of fortune left him feeling overwhelmed.

How long had they suspected Cassie? Why didn't they share their suspicions with me?

The answer struck him like a thunderbolt. *They didn't know if one of us had been influenced by her little trick. Any one of us could have been…could still be her puppet.*

Deacon knew one thing for certain: nothing would ever be the same again. *We can't kill these people; we need a way of undoing her hold.*

Epilogue

Jennifer Polar

Jenniger goes shopping

The sun-drenched streets of Beverly Hills were eerily quiet, save for the shuffling of feet and the occasional guttural growl. Jennifer Polar, resplendent in a designer evening gown that seemed absurdly out of place, pushed a shopping cart through the crowded aisles of a long-abandoned supermarket. Growlers shuffled past her, their milky eyes ignoring her, their rotting flesh a contrast to her pristine appearance.

With casual indifference, Jennifer plucked tins and packets of dried foods from the shelves, tossing them into her cart. A growler bumped against her, leaving a smear of black ooze on her gown. She tsked, brushing at the stain with manicured nails.

Back at her mansion, its roof gleaming with solar panels, Jennifer checked the well pump before heading inside. The door closed behind her, shutting out the apocalyptic world beyond. In the cavernous kitchen, she popped the cork on a bottle of champagne, the sound echoing through the empty halls.

Steam rose from the opulent bathroom as she lowered herself into a bubble bath, champagne flute in hand. She closed her eyes, savoring the warmth and the crisp taste of the bubbly.

Later, she lounged by the oversized pool, her skin glistening with tanning oil. The California sun beat down, unaware that the world had ended.

"What do you want, Samual?" she asked irritably as a man emerged from the mansion, disturbing her peace.

"Your sister needs your help," he replied, his tone neutral but urgent.

Jennifer sat up and gave a weary sigh. "Cassie needs *my* help? Can't her husband help?"

"He is working the European theater."

A flicker of interest crossed Jennifer's face. "My sister's problem, does it have anything to do with the loss of our California horde?"

"Yes, ma'am."

“I thought it would have something to do with her. Does Mr. LaCroix know?”

Samual shook his head. “It would not be prudent to inform him. You know how he gets.”

Jennifer's lips curved into a smirk. “Well, she likes that kind of thing.”

Samual did not grin in response. "She said if she wasn't heard from for three days, you are to bring mayhem to the bunker."

"Santa Rosa? Our bunker?" Jennifer shook her head in wonder.

"Well," Jennifer purred, standing up and stretching languidly, "I guess we can start by unlocking the cocooning chamber. That'll probably kill anyone who isn't imprinted, which means everyone but Cassie and her people."

"Yes, ma'am."

"Then I guess we bring in the troops now that we know where the so-called secret entrance is."

"Yes, ma'am."

Jennifer's eyes glittered with malicious anticipation. "Oh, and Samual? Tell the boys to prep my ride. It's been far too long since I've had some real fun."

Samual nodded. "Ma'am, is it possible the President will nuke the bunker now that he knows the notorious Samantha Winters and her followers are there? Or at least launch his own invasion."

Jennifer snickered. "There's no chance he'll nuke it. What's buried underneath that bunker is the whole point of the outbreak: a treasure beyond all treasures. As for invading it, if the Marines had not broken the chain of command, he would have retaken the bunker already, but he's lost 95% of the military to the Black, to the growlers, and to rebellion. He will be busy for a while building his great new Satanic theocracy."

Samual nodded and retreated into the house. Jennifer turned her gaze toward the horizon, where the faint outlines of shuffling growlers could be seen. A slow, wicked smile spread across her face.

"Ready or not, big sister," she murmured, "Santa Rosa, here I come."

THE END

THANK YOU!

Thank you so much for reading *The Growler Chronicles: Book 5 – Paradise Falls*. I truly hope you enjoyed the adventure and that you'll continue to follow along as the journey unfolds in the next book.

If you loved this book, it would mean the world to me if you could take a moment to leave a **five-star review** on Amazon. Your reviews help other readers discover the series and allow me to keep writing the stories you love.

Thank you for your support, and see you in the next installment!

Stay safe, and keep surviving!

Coming Soon The Growler Chronicles: Book 6 - Hellfire

THANK YOU!

Made in the USA
Middletown, DE
04 December 2024